BRIDE BY CONTRACT

Troy Belvoir walked into Lady Morva's life and took it over. But just why had he married her? Was she really just part of a business contract? Or did his marriage vows mean something to him?

Books you will enjoy
by MARGARET ROME

RAPTURE OF THE DEEP

The disagreeable Leon Casson, Director of Operations on a huge Shetland oil rig, had not wanted Catriona Dunross as his secretary— and she had only taken the job because family commitments had forced her hand; but there they were, stuck with each other. In the ensuing fight, who would win?

LORD OF THE LAND

Frances had only gone to Andalucia to try to finish the book her father had been writing before he died, and she hoped to enlist the help of the local grandee, the aloof Conde Romanes de los Nomandos y Aguila. But he, it soon turned out, required something in return from her. . . .

BAY OF ANGELS

In Cannes during the Film Festival week, with an ambitious actress friend, poor Cherry was feeling thoroughly out of her depth. She was neither an actress nor ambitious, and all she wanted was to get away. So it was particularly unfortunate that the saturnine Lucien Tarascon, Duc de Marchiel, should have got entirely the wrong impression of her. . . .

CASTLE OF THE LION

Really Petra only had herself to blame that her spoilt young brother had landed himself in serious trouble in Cyprus and was calling for her to come and get him out of it. And the only man who could help her was the stern Stelios Heracles—and Petra was the only one who could pay his price. . . .

BRIDE BY CONTRACT

BY

MARGARET ROME

MILLS & BOON LIMITED
15–16 BROOK'S MEWS
LONDON W1A 1DR

First published in Great Britain 1984
by Mills & Boon Limited

© Margaret Rome 1984

Australian copyright 1984
Philippine copyright 1984
This edition 1984

ISBN 0 263 74876 6

Set in Monophoto Plantin 10 on 11½ pt.
01-1284 – 48970

Made and printed in Great Britain by
Richard Clay (The Chaucer Press) Ltd,
Bungay, Suffolk

CHAPTER ONE

A MIST had descended, a fine grey stole that had wreathed around the gently sloping shoulders, curved mounds and plunging depths of the Cumbrian Fells, rendering them invisible. The wild, deserted terrain made up of bleak moorland, peat bog, gritstone and rain-drenched heather might have been purposely designed to discourage strangers from lingering, a hermitage of a place that could appeal only to its inhabitants—to herds of horned sheep in the charge of taciturn shepherds; to ravens that clung tenaciously to their territory, refusing to be ousted by the dry, cold Helm Wind; to rabbits and red grouse, partridge and pheasant, and to the girl who sat slumped in a saddle allowing her sure-footed mare to amble homeward at its own chosen place.

When Morva sighed the mare pricked up her ears and whinnied as if anxious to convey sympathy to the constant companion whose confidences she was accustomed to sharing.

'The whole countryside seems to be aware of our loss, Clio,' she mused sadly. 'Do you suppose the skies are weeping, the clouds hanging low, the birds silent and the animals still because they too are mourning Daddy's death?'

Clio trembled to a standstill, her head drooping lower as her rider's sad dialogue continued.

'William Arthur Percy Eden, Earl of Howgill, Viscount Bowderdale, died as he had lived—quietly, unceremoniously, causing as little upset as possible to his servants and to members of his family. He was all alone in his study,' she winced, 'seated at the desk where he had spent so many hours, months and years studying his beloved books, when he simply closed his eyes and drifted out of a life rendered joyless since the day Mummy walked out on him, enticed by the flattery and costly bribes of a wealthier but very much older man. Even so, after all this time, I think I might have found it possible to have forgiven her even that,' Morva concluded huskily, 'if only she had shown respect for father's memory by attending his funeral. . . .'

Clio's head jerked up, responding to a sudden tug upon the reins as her rider shuddered from delving too deeply into the motives of a mother capable of deserting a faithful husband, the handsome, grown-up son she had professed to adore, and an infant daughter, conceived on impulse to alleviate the boredom of approaching middle age, then abandoned without a qualm when romance had swept into her life, offering a tempting prospect of thrills, excitement and rejuvenation.

Suddenly anxious to be freed of thoughts as desolate and unproductive as the surrounding moorland, Morva dug her heels lightly into Clio's flanks and headed her in the direction of a road winding downhill through woodland to a fertile valley; passing grazing cattle, cultivated fields, over a humped-back bridge, then rising steeply towards the huge scrolled and crested gates of Ravenscrag Castle, family seat of the Earls of Howgill.

The mist had developed into steadily drizzling rain by the time she had cantered Clio through the castle's parkland, skirted formal gardens, then headed for the rear of an ancient edifice built of local grey stone that appeared to have been sculpted from, rather than erected against, its rocky backdrop. Seconds after they passed beneath a stone archway the sound of hooves clattering against the stone-flagged stable yard alerted a groom, who hurried out of the stables to help Morva dismount.

'You're wanted in the library, milady,' he informed her urgently. 'Lady Howgill, Viscount Bowderdale, and Mister Kingsale have been waiting ages!'

Morva clasped a guilty hand to her mouth. Mister Kingsale, her father's solicitor! How *could* she have forgotten her grandmother's strict injunction not to be late for the reading of the Will!

Her distressed blush caused the groom's features to twist into a grimace of sympathy for the girl whose peculiar upbringing was a constant source of discussion below stairs. Noting a look akin to panic in large brown eyes that put him in mind of a frightened doe, the slight trembling of a full, sensitively curved mouth, and the worried gesture of fingers combing through a glistening sweep of beech-brown hair clinched at the nape of a childishly slender neck by plastic bobbles, he wondered if Cook could have been right in her withering condemnation of the Dowager Countess of Howgill.

'Lady Howgill should never have been allowed a free hand in the upbringing of her granddaughter,' she had insisted, 'the age discrepancy is too great! Ever since the day the Countess took over the supervision of the nursery, almost eighteen years ago, she's bullied the poor bairn into submission, moulded her like a piece of clay into her own image of how a young lady should look and behave, turned her into a replica of the prim, rigidly hidebound young ladies who've been bred solely with the marriage market in mind ever since the aristocracy came into existence. The old Countess's ideas are a century out of date,' she had snorted. 'How I pity the bairn—the combination of a solitary upbringing and her grandmother's strong influence has rendered Lady Morva unmarriageable in this day and age!'

'The Countess will find her a husband, don't you fret,' a young footman had laconically contributed. 'Circumstances haven't changed much over the years. However much the upper classes may strive to appear in sympathy with modern day notions of female emancipation and an individual's right to personal freedom, we can see evidence all around us that the aristocracy's breeding programme is still going strong. Colts may have been allowed to kick over a few more traces; fillies may have been granted a longer rein, nevertheless,' his lips had twisted into a cynical smile, 'having been reared from birth to accept purity of bloodstock as their first priority, the majority eventually respond to the crack of the family whip. Take Viscount Bowderdale as an example! The whole of London society is aware of his liking for slender, leggy blondes, yet his West Country fiancée is typical of the sturdy-thighed, broad-beamed huntin', shootin' and fishin' set!'

The titter of laughter that had run around the table had aroused Cook's intense family loyalty.

'Obviously, Lord Percy feels himself duty bound to do everything in his power to redeem the family fortune. Ravenscrag is crammed with costly treasures but unfortunately everything is entailed and death duties are bound to reduce his financial inheritance to a mere pittance.'

'Thank goodness everything *is* entailed, otherwise he'd have the contents of the castle under the auctioneer's hammer in less time than it takes to put up an "Antique Auction" sign,' a gardener had sourly observed.

'Yet he'll survive!' another servant had cut in dryly. 'He's his mother's son, that one, determined to ensure that he gets the best out of life whoever does the paying!'

A unanimous chorus of assent had almost drowned Cook's sober reflection.

'I just hope that the late Earl has made ample provisions for his daughter, that his quiet, simple unmercenary nature will not turn out to be the sum total of her inheritance.'

Happily unaware of the groom's train of thought, Morva appealed in a breathless rush.

'Would you look after Clio, please, Thomas? Make certain she gets a good rub down and put a fresh supply of drinking water into her trough. But leave the grooming, I'll do it myself after the meeting. I shouldn't be away more than half an hour.'

Schooling herself not to break into a run, conscious of her duty to set an example of dignity and grace to any watching servants, Morva hurried into the castle. The exaggerated sound made by the heels of her riding boots upon the chequered marble floor of the Great Hall caused her to wince, expecting any moment to hear her grandmother's voice haranguing her lack of social grace as she made panic-stricken progress towards huge double doors leading into the library.

In common with most of the rooms inside the castle,

the interior was so huge and spacious she was able to
to slip quietly inside and stand for a few moments
unobserved while she recovered her equilibrium. The
long, narrow room lined with books from floor to
ceiling, with a staircase in one corner leading up to a
gallery lined with a rail of mosaic gold, seemed heavy
with an atmosphere that felt oppressive. Quickly, she
scanned mahogany sofas and chairs; numerous brasses
and *objets d'art*; the leather spines and gilt titles of
books which normally projected an aura of comfort
and calm, seeking a reason for the presentiment of
trouble that had disturbed her senses.

Her feeling of unease increased as she advanced
farther into the room and saw her brother Percy,
whose features she had never before seen disturbed by
so much as a frown, standing white-faced, apparently
frozen to immobility. Then she saw their family
solicitor, the usually urbane Mister Kingsale, looking
flushed with embarrassment as he attempted to
console her grandmother who had shrivelled into an
armchair and was actually *weeping in public*!

'Granny, whatever's wrong?' Forgetting years of
social training, she ran the length of the library and
dropped to her knees beside the regal, stately old
Countess who placed pride and deportment high upon
her list of priorities. But for the first time in living
memory strong emotion had crashed with the force of
a tidal wave through the old lady's defences, rendering
her a frail human wreck, completely overwhelmed by
strong emotional currents.

'Percy ...? Mister Kingsale ...?' Morvan's
shocked brown eyes begged for enlightenment. 'What
have you been saying to cause Granny such dreadful
upset?'

When both men stared mutely, and no immediate response seemed forthcoming, she rose from her knees to slip an arm around her grandmother's frail shoulders, at the same time attempting to prise away the hands shielding her wrinkled, tear-stained cheeks.

'Granny, you must stop crying or you'll make yourself ill!' Morva pleaded on a note of fear. 'I'm certain that whoever is responsible for your tears had no intention of being deliberately hurtful.'

'No, of course he had not!' She barely recognised the harsh voice grating from her brother's lips. 'Father was incapable of deliberate action—ambiguity, vagueness, evasion, yes, but apparently straightforward honesty was more than the ninth Earl of Howgill could handle!'

Morva stared, shocked speechless by the treacherous tirade aimed at the father who had indulged his only son to the point of satiety, granting his every wish, indulging his every whim, heaping upon his heir excessive evidence of love and kindness.

'How can you say such things!' she finally managed to stammer. 'You, of all people! Small wonder Granny is so upset if she has been made to listen to such ... *sacrilegious* statements!'

'Please, I beg of you,' Mister Kingsale attempted to take charge, 'no more recriminations, we must all make an effort to remain calm, to seek some way out of an extremely shocking and embarrassing situation. If you would kindly be seated, Lady Morva. And you, Lord ... er ... Percy.'

Much to Morva's puzzlement their solicitor's complexion turned brick red.

'Lady Howgill,' hastily he turned to address her quietly sobbing grandmother, 'do you wish to acquaint your granddaughter with the contents of the late Earl of Howgill's letter, or shall I?'

Interpreting the limp wave of her hand as permission to carry on, Mister Kingsale sat down next to Morva and took pity on her bewilderment by placing her suddenly trembling hands between steady, comforting palms.

'I wish I could find a way of saving you from distress, Lady Morva,' he began gently, 'but for the sake of your grandmother and brother who are already in a state of shock my explanation has to be brief and blunt.'

Morva froze, feeling a stirring of fear, conscious of her brother's shoulders squaring as he stood staring out of the window, of a small choking sob coming from the direction of the chair where her grandmother sat huddled, looking every one of her eighty-odd years.

'In order to avert the possibility of my unpleasant duty becoming too prolonged, I must ask you, Lady Morva, to listen without interruption, to save any questions or remarks until later.'

When Morva withdrew her hands from his to place them, fists tightly bunched, in her lap, he nodded approval of this sign of courage and continued gravely.

'I was instructed by your father when last we met, to hand a sealed envelope to your brother before the reading of the Will. If I had been given the faintest inkling of what the envelope contained I would have given it to your brother in private so that he would have had time to assimilate its shocking contents before having to face his family. As it was,' he sighed regretfully, 'receiving the news as he did was a doubly cruel blow.'

Morva wanted to move, wanted to signal a message of sympathy and forgiveness to her stricken brother, but her limbs were held rigid, her eyes fixed, teeming with trepidation.

'The envelope contained a letter and two legal documents.' Mr Kingsale's voice quickened, adopting the speed and precision of one forced to accept responsibility for defusing an unexploded bomb. 'A marriage certificate stating details of your father's marriage to Grace Rhoda Allen, spinster—your mother's maiden name, of course—and dated the sixth day of September, nineteen hundred and forty-five. Also a second certificate,' he cleared his throat before hurrying on, 'showing details of the birth of a son, Percy, to William Arthur Percy Eden and Grace Rhoda Allen on the first day of September, nineteen hundred and forty-four.'

For long, bewildered seconds Morva's sluggish brain struggled to make sense of the information it had been given, sifting the facts, searching the debris for the bombshell she had been braced to expect. But there was no shock of explosion, just the fizzling of a damp squib. Fear faded from her eyes as almost angrily she accused the anxiety-ridden solicitor.

'Is that all?' Her amazed glance slid from her motionless brother to her wilting grandmother then back to the solicitor. 'The fact that my brother was born a year before our parents were married would scarcely raise an eyebrow in this enlightened age.'

The eruption she had been dreading came from the spot where her brother stood. With a bellow of anger he turned on his heel to stride towards her, bending to glower a look of frustration over her bewildered face.

'Can't you see farther than the end of your nose,

you stupid little fool? I was born before our parents were married which means that I am illegitimate! Illegitimate sons are barred from inheriting a title, so as the earldom of Howgill does not descend in the female line, the title, together with Ravenscrag Castle, its contents and surrounding estate, will become the inheritance of some stranger at present unknown who will inevitably want the present occupants turfed out of his future home!'

The air had cleared, the dust had settled, yet, Morva reflected as she glanced at the other two occupants of Granny's small sitting room, they were all three reacting like victims of shell shock, speaking and moving in a daze, with eyes glazed, emotions stunned into a state comparable with the effect of an anaesthetic injected into a patient whose limb was about to be amputated. Her grandmother had recovered to the extent of insisting that they should act out the charade of eating dinner.

'The servants must be given no grounds to suspect that anything is amiss,' she had insisted with a mere trace of her usual firmness. 'We must carry on as usual until——' she had swallowed hard then continued bravely, 'the new Earl of Howgill arrives.'

'Thank you, Buchan.' Vaguely Morva's mind registered the fact that her grandmother was dismissing the hovering butler. 'Lady Morva will pour out the coffee; you may leave us now.'

Somehow, Morva forced her limbs to respond to the implied command, picking up the heavy silver coffee pot, willing her hands not to tremble as she poured drinks no one wanted into eggshell china cups.

'None for me, thank you, Morva,' Percy declined,

'I prefer brandy. Would either of you care to join me?'

'No, thank you, Percy.' Morva shook her head, her heart racing with pride on behalf of her brother who was trying so hard to display the courage of an officer and a gentleman. She loved him so much, she acknowledged with an inner ache, the brother who was eighteen years her senior, who had sauntered in and out of her life like a handsome, golden-haired god, patting her head in passing, bringing her occasional presents that had been treasured and carefully stored. . . .

'We will both join you, Percy, dear.' Arbitrarily, her grandmother overruled Morva's refusal. 'There are decisions to be made, plans to be drawn up—a liqueur will help to release tension so allowing concentration to be more easily achieved.'

Morva waited until their drinks had been poured and Percy had returned to his seat before blurting out the questions she had been too shocked to ask in Mister Kingsale's presence.

'What I cannot understand is how Percy could have been born without your knowledge, Granny! And why weren't the circumstances surrounding his birth made known to him years ago? It was criminal of Daddy to sllow him to believe that he was destined to become the tenth Earl of Howgill, to wait until the last possible moment before snatching away what he had been brought up to regard as his rightful inheritance!'

Bleakly, her grandmother responded. 'The answer to your first question is that, in nineteen forty-four, the year in which Percy was born, our country was at war. Your father, in common with the majority of young men of his generation, had been called into active service and during the four years he was serving with his regiment he paid just a few flying visits home.

'Naturally, I was displeased, yet I could not bring myself to condemn a young soldier living a life of constant danger for wanting to relax, to tour the fun-spots of the capital in the company of his fellow officers. I believe that it was in London, during his last leave before his regiment embarked to take part in the invasion of Normandy, that he and your mother first met. A year later, when he brought his family home to Ravenscrag. I was given no reason to suspect that the girl he introduced as his wife was, in fact, his very recent bride.'

Gravely Morva pondered on her grandmother's explanation, conscious of the dislike that had existed, the antagonism that had flowed between the old and the new Countess of Howgill. She had no recollection of her mother, she knew her only as a word-portrait painted by her grandmother in strokes of scarlet and vermilion—with a dense black void where her heart should have been.

'The answer to your second question is contained in Father's letter.' Percy patted his breast pocket as if having to convince himself that the document really did exist, that the events of the past few hours were not just a part of some intolerable nightmare. 'He begins by apologising for his sin of omission,' his lips twisted into a grimace of wry resentment, 'excusing his lapse, in the first instance, on the grounds of his being unable to resist mother's tearful pleading not to reveal their secret. Then secondly, after their divorce had been finalised, because he could not bear the thought of having to face the anger and contempt of a son who had been made to feel confident of his role in society.'

Morva almost cried out in pain when suddenly he bowed his head to rake agitated fingers through his hair.

'Granny!' he groaned, 'what am I to do with my life? I realise that I must resign my commission and, of course, break off my engagement——'

'For heaven's sake, *why* . . .?' Morva jumped to her feet, blinded by a sudden surge of tears. 'Wh . . . what does the lack of a title matter to two people who are in love?' Fiercely, she brushed away her tears, missing the look of helpless resignation passing between her brother and grandmother. 'Please don't rush into hasty decisions, Percy,' she gulped. 'Who knows, it may be months—even years—before the new Earl of Howgill can be found!'

'If you had had sufficient grace to have made your appearance at the appointed time, you would be aware that information concerning the whereabouts of your father's successor was included in his letter,' her grandmother snapped with the asperity of one who had almost reached the end of her tether. 'The person's name is Belvoir—Troy Belvoir,' she stressed with a fastidious shudder. 'Mister Kingsale has intimated that he intends writing to inform his new client of his inheritance this very day; I have no doubt whatsoever that he will descend upon us just as quickly as he is able to arrange transportation from his shack in the Canadian Rockies!'

CHAPTER TWO

MORVA reined Clio to a standstill the moment she spotted the chocolate-brown limousine parked before the steps leading up to the main entrance to the castle. For amazed seconds her eyes roved over the gleaming bodywork, tinted windows, plump, white-walled tyres and opulent cream leather upholstery of what appeared to her to be the longest and most expensive car in the world. Who could it belong to? In spite of the fact that Percy could number quite a few millionaires amongst his friends, she felt certain that not one member of his aristocratic set would descend to flaunting such an ostentatious, even vulgar, display of wealth.

Tantalised by curiosity, she wheeled Clio in the direction of the stables and quickly dismounted, leaving her in the charge of a stable boy before making her way towards the West Wing where Granny's small sitting room was situated. But the pleasantly furnished room with its deep wooden windowseats, shelved recesses strewn with a collection of Victorian bric-a-brac, and two huge leather chairs with outspread arms placed within toe-toasting distance of the fireplace, was empty. It was the only habitable room in the castle during the early morning hours, the only one that was free of draughts blowing chilly as the Helm Wind along unheated stone passageways.

With increasing curiosity she went in search of her

grandmother and her unusual visitor, tripping lightly up the handsome West Staircase towards more formal apartments in which important visitors were received—important only in the sense that her grandmother wished them to be impressed with the full grandeur of her stately surroundings. The moment she opened the door of the Blue Drawing Room the sound of her grandmother's cultured slightly condescending voice proved her suspicion correct. Whoever it was that had been granted an audience within the imposing surroundings of walls lined with dark blue Indian silk; tall windows with wooden swags covered in the same exotic material; eighteenth-century footstools, sofas and tables that had been commissioned by the fifth Earl; a collection of priceless family portraits painted by famous artists; silver-framed mirrors and bronze and ormolu urns, was being subjected to the full blast of her grandmother's *grand dame* treatment. Prepared to act as rescuer Morva stepped quietly into the room, but her pleasant smile of welcome froze on her lips when she heard the visitor respond to some remark of her grandmother's in a mildly amused, but definitely *Transatlantic* drawl.

'During my early youth I dabbled in dozens of occupations, Lady Howgill—forest ranger; ranchhand; cowboy; surveyor; blacksmith; elk hunter; horse wrangler; itinerant—you name a place, and I've most likely been there—but when my father died ten years ago I was forced to settle down to running the family business.'

Standing still and unobserved, Morva took wide-eyed stock of the stranger she guessed instinctively was the usurper, the man who, because of loyalty owing to her brother, she felt duty-bound to dislike—the new Earl of Howgill.

He was huge. A typical product of his natural environment, a place whose geography she had been studying during weeks spent awaiting his arrival, where mountains rose two miles higher than the level of the ocean; where cottonwood trees grew tall; precipices dropped to the depth of eternity, where the landscape was so turbulent it defied description—rock slides and ridges, steeples and crags, snowfields and canyons, streams alive with trout, gulches harbouring gold and silver ore, forests that were home to gophers, marmot, coyotes, and the huge, lumbering, deceptively cuddly-looking grizzly bear. . . .

She had just begun edging silently towards the door, beset by uncertainty and the shyness that had plagued her since childhood, when her grandmother's gimlet eyes swivelled towards her. Immediately, she cut short her visitor's good-humoured confidences.

'How very interesting! Later, you must tell me more, but now you must meet my granddaughter.' Imperiously she beckoned. 'Come here, child!

She waited impatiently until Morva crept nearer.

'Lady Morva Eden—the Most Honourable Earl of Howgill.' She effected the introduction with a distinct sneer.

Morva had to tip back her head to meet the friendly gaze of clear, bright eyes that looked used to scanning distant horizons, capturing in their depths the reflection of skies that were cloudless, serene, and deep cobalt blue.

'Glad to make your acquaintance, Lady Eden!'

Nervously, she nodded acknowledgment, brushing cool fingertips over a palm that felt powerful as a paw, then hastily withdrawing her hand from his threatened crushing clasp. Too shy to return his keen scrutiny, her glance slid away from dense black hair curled tightly as the fleece of a close-shorn ram, down the crags and crevices of his sun- and wind-tanned profile, passed startlingly white teeth and a jutting jawline to come to rest upon a chequered shirt stretched taut across muscular shoulders, a massive chest, and sinuously moving biceps.

Her eyes were running scared, panicky as a doe on unknown territory, yet he apparently mistook her furtive reconnaissance for a condemning stare.

'I guess I should apologise for my informal gear.' She followed his rueful glance down towards casual shoes and rangy limbs encased in pale blue cords. 'I didn't know quite what I'd find at the end of my journey. To be honest,' he caught her unawares with a wide, engaging grin, 'I set off for Ravenscrag expecting to have to clamber over ancient ruins.'

Before Morva could answer, her grandmother's hard, unforgiving voice intruded.

'Then how gratified you must have felt, Lord Howgill, when you discovered that far from inheriting an empty title you were the present custodian of one of England's stateliest homes housing a priceless collection of medieval and Renaissance art, to say nothing of a thriving estate, three thousand acres of land with eight tenant farms, and a forty-acre lake!'

The interloper appeared disappointingly unimpressed.

'I could have been knocked down with the proverbial feather,' he shrugged, his broad width of shoulders making an incongruous contradiction of his words. 'Really, Lady Howgill, I can't quite see myself as a belted earl. In fact, my friends back home fell about laughing when they heard of my elevation to the English peerage.'

'Indeed!' Lady Howgill's imperious nostrils flared. 'And do *you* also view the honourable title you have inherited as a source of vulgar amusement?'

Morva flinched, feeling sympathy for the new earl whose unsophisticated background had rendered him ill-equipped to withstand her grandmother's crushing weight of displeasure. She looked away, fixing her eyes upon the carpet as, with fists tightly clenched, she shared his feeling of cowed embarrassment, the sense of inadequacy her grandmother was capable of inflicting with just a few disdainful words.

But his response, though softly drawled, was far from abject. Indeed, to Morva's shocked ears, he sounded as if he was daring to mildly censure a wilful octogenarian for her petulant, ill-mannered remark.

'My friends are not vulgar, ma'am, they're merely frank, friendly, big-hearted Canadians who've missed out on the benefits of a privileged upbringing, who have no accepted rules of behaviour other than an innate courtesy that demands that visitors should be made welcome and put fully at their ease, together with a belief that the essence of good manners is consideration for the feelings of others—a sensibility that comes naturally to some but which appears to demand considerable effort from an unfortunate few.'

Her grandmother's outraged gasp provided ample evidence that his lightly barbed reproach had landed directly on target, shattering the composure of the Countess who took pride in showing an example of fine breeding, irreproachable etiquette, and exemplary manners.

'Well, really . . .!'

When her grandmother lapsed into outraged silence Morva had to fight an almost irresistible urge to applaud the unlikely winner of a joust—a tilting match of words—in which the most experienced contestant had been cleverly outmanoeuvred. Unwilling admiration for the quiet-spoken Canadian grew when he attempted to placate his stiffly held, angrily flushed adversary.

'I can understand why I must appear like a sneak thief in the corral to you and your family,' he consoled gently, 'but believe me, I'm no mountain varmint preparing to pounce on a defenceless doe.'

Morva sensed rather than glimpsed his clear blue gaze swivelling towards the space above her downbent head, but when she looked up he was once more addressing her keenly listening grandmother.

'I know nothing of protocol and pageantry, or of the sort of conduct expected of peers of the realm. And as business affairs eat up great chunks of my time I have no wish to take on further responsibilities. The Earldom of Howgill rightfully belongs to your grandson,' he stressed with what sounded to Morva like a hint of desperation. 'Surely a way can be found to prevent the title from passing to a very distant relative?'

'There are no ties of blood between our two families, Lord Howgill,' her grandmother disclaimed with a haste that was almost insulting. 'You have succeeded to the earldom because you are the nearest male descendant of a former holder of the title. And no,' she confessed with a weary, regretful sigh, 'there is no way round the rare and curious situation that has resulted in my grandson being robbed of his expectations. Letters patent granted to the first Lord Howgill specify that only legitimate offspring can inherit the title. My grandson was born almost a year before his parents were married, therefore nothing can be done to put him in line to the title. The best peerage lawyer in the land was consulted. His conclusion was most definite. The Legitimacy Act excludes illegitimate children from inheriting a peerage!'

When her grandmother dabbed at her eyes with a dainty lace handkerchief Morva cast her a suspicious glance, wondering what tricks were being secreted up the sleeve of the haughty old aristocrat who never apologised, never explained, and had certainly never been known to angle for sympathy.

'As you can imagine,' she appealed, twisting the scrap of lace into an agitated ball, 'the news came as a great shock not only to Percy—who was, of course, the greatest loser—but also to my granddaughter and myself who have known no other home but Ravenscrag Castle.' As if having to draw upon pitiable reserves of courage she tilted her chin, yet still managed to portray an image of a frail, broken spirit when she concluded in a barely audible whisper.

'We delayed our departure in order to extend a personal welcome to the new owner of Ravenscrag. Now that you have arrived, I shall instruct the servants to begin packing our belongings immediately.'

With foxes one must play the fox! The old country maxim flashed through Morva's mind as she stood transfixed, watching the effect of her grandmother's cunningly dangled bait upon the unsuspecting quarry possessing an ample endowment of virility and strength yet who appeared blind to the presence of hidden snares.

'No need to act hastily.' Awkwardly he stumbled into her grandmother's trap. 'I would consider it an honour, ma'am, if you and Lady Morva would stay and keep me company for as long as you find it convenient.'

'How very generous!' Traitorously, Morva found herself comparing her grandmother's smile with the baring of complacent fangs. 'My granddaughter and I will be glad to delay our departure so as to assist you in any way we can to adjust to your new role in society, Lord. . . .'

She hesitated, pouting doubtfully. 'Oh dear! If we are to continue living under the same roof we must try to be a little less formal. If you wish, you may address me as Lady Lucy. But how am I to address you?'

'Why not call me Troy?' His relieved grin encompassed Morva as well as her grandmother. 'I was landed with the name simply because I happened to be born on the anniversary of the day my great grandpa found his first sizeable nugget.'

'Ah yes, I do see the connection! Troy measure is used to weigh precious metals, is it not?' She smiled politely, then shook her head. 'No, I think I prefer Belvoir—pronounced *Bee*ver, of course . . .?'

The new earl looked astonished. 'How on earth did you know? I've always regarded the unusual pronunciation as a family quirk!'

'Not at all, dear boy,' she deigned to bestow a patronising smile, 'it is the proper English pronunciation. I'm relieved to discover that whatever else your ancestor may have left behind when he emigrated to Canada, his proud family name travelled with him.'

'Very well,' he conceded with a grin. 'I don't mind your using my surname if that is what you prefer. Actually, it's rather apt. My friends insist that I work like a beaver! I take all such remarks as compliments— the busy beaver can fell a fully grown tree and strip it of bark and branches simply by using its teeth.'

'Is that the sort of work you do, felling trees?' The question popped out before Morva could stop it. For the first time in her life she was experiencing intense curiosity about a member of the opposite sex, a man so entirely different from the few of her brother's friends who had occasionally paid them a visit that he appeared to her not just as a visitor from a Commonwealth country, but as a creature from another planet—a planet inhabited by males who grew tall and straight as trees, who had muscular bodies built as if specially designed to withstand the rigours of the great outdoors, fists fashioned to mould around the handles of razor-edged choppers; rippling, power-packed shoulder muscles; lithe, agile limbs to enable them to shin up trees or to keep a massive frame perfectly balanced upon slippery, newly felled tree trunks inching downriver towards nearby sawmills.

When he trained his eyes in her direction she shrank inwardly, wishing the impulsive question had never been allowed to edge his firm mouth with a crinkle of amusement; to invite a look that was keen, tolerant, and puzzlingly kind, the sort of look usually reserved for children and for very young animals too timid to explore their surroundings, too unprepared for life to be separated from their family.

'Some of the happiest years of my youth were spent as a lumberjack,' he confirmed her theory, 'but these days,' he ran rueful fingers through a thick black

fleece of hair, 'I spend most of my time behind a desk;
sitting inside stuffy offices and conference rooms;
rushing to airports, working during flights, conclud-
ing a deal, then rushing all the way back again. There
are drawbacks to being an only child,' he confessed. 'I
delegate as much authority as I deem wise, nevertheless, it would be nice to have a brother or sister to help
lighten the load.'

Morva's eyes widened, startled by the unexpected
revelation of wealth and status. But her grandmother's
reaction was almost comically riveting.

'When you referred to a family business, Belvoir, I
formed an opinion that you were somehow connected
with trade . . .?'

'With numerous trades,' he corrected casually.
Then to her intense annoyance he allowed himself to
become side-tracked, waiting until Morva had relaxed
on to a sofa before following her example and gingerly
easing his bulk into a spindle-legged chair. His
expression of relief when it gave no indication of
collapsing beneath his weight was so amusing Morva
was forced to choke back a giggle, knowing that the
least hint of levity would incur her grandmother's
frown of displeasure.

'Please do go on!' her grandmother prompted when
he relaxed with his long legs stuck well out in front of
him, apparently in no hurry to appease her curiosity.
'I'd be most interested to learn more of your family
history.'

'It's not half so interesting as your own, Lady
Lucy.' His eyes had adopted a cobalt blue twinkle.
'But if you insist . . .?'

'I do,' she pressed, dismissing her usual decorum
far enough to lean forward in anticipation.

'Well,' he obliged, in an unhurried, almost lazy drawl, 'for some reason known only to himself, my grandpa emigrated to Canada sometime around the mid-nineteenth century. He headed straight for the Rocky Mountains, bought a shovel and a pack mule, and for the following few years tramped from one prospectors' site to another in search of pay dirt. At times he must have felt terribly disheartened, striking a little gold here, a little silver there, but never raising sufficient colour in his pail to do more than replace his depleted provisions.

'Most ores were played out, most mining camps had been abandoned, by the time he found his Eldorado— nuggets the size of hens' eggs scattered along the bed of a stream that had been supplying him with drinking water!'

'He was a bachelor at that time, I suppose?' Lady Lucy posed the question Morva was too spellbound to ask.

'He sure was. Wives were looked upon as a liability in pay dirt country. But he wasted no time at all remedying that omission. Once he'd registered his claim and bought himself a suit, he went looking for a young, healthy wife to bear his children. As luck would have it, she bore him only one, but that one was sufficient to ensure that the Belvoir dynasty could begin to grow.'

'And did it grow?' Her grandmother's sharp, terse question caused Morva to jump.

'It grew and grew,' he affirmed, his voice echoing with the assurance of a race which, unlike the British, saw no shame in boasting of successes, in advertising achievement—saw no point at all in making money if one was not prepared to flaunt it. 'Our assets include oil wells in America; banks in Toronto; a sheep station in Australia; offices in Toronto, London and New York, not to mention grandpa's original gold contracts and investments in sterling.'

'Then you must be a millionaire!' Morva barely recognised her grandmother's voice tinged with an unusual note of awe. 'Perhaps even a multi-millionaire . . .?'

'We . . . ll, Lady Lucy,' he smiled, 'as to that, I really couldn't say.' His nut-brown features became split with a wide, teasing grin. 'Where I come from we have a saying: "A man can't be counted rich if he can count his money!"'

'How utterly unjust life can be!' The statement jerked from Morva's lips, riveting her grandmother to her seat, causing the Earl's vivid blue eyes to narrow then cloud darkly as skies gathering around a mountain peak. The realisation that her remark must have sounded envious, even snobbish, released a rush of shamed colour into her cheeks.

'Forgive me, it was not my intention to sound offensive,' she mumbled, wishing that the multi-flowered carpet were a garden into which she could flee to hide her shame. Conscious of two pairs of eyes demanding an explanation, she attempted a blundering justification.

'It's just that . . . I couldn't help comparing the Belvoir family's exorbitant rewards with the pitiable returns achieved by my own and many other aristocratic families who are struggling against impossible odds. The high cost of living in stately homes has forced many to move out of huge country houses into small farmhouses. Art treasures, and even whole estates, are having to be sold in order to pay death duties, and some peers have even been forced into exile because they've been unable to meet crippling tax bills. Daddy must have worked every bit as hard as you have, Lord Howgill,' she gulped, unable to force a less formal form of address past her lips, 'yet Ravenscrag continued to be a drain upon his resources. Even during good years, the estate lost thousands of pounds, in spite of overheads having been cut to the bone. Perhaps it's just as well that you are a wealthy man,' she warned a trifle bitterly, 'considering the fact that the rates bill alone is more than five thousand pounds a year.'

'You say your father worked hard,' he encouraged sympathetically. 'Which chore placed the most strain upon his time, d'you reckon, Lady Morva?'

'Doing the estate books.'

'Writing endless poetry!' her grandmother snapped in unison.

Morva resented the way his expression changed from tolerant to faintly cynical, hated the dry note of censure in his voice when he dared to sit in judgment upon her late father.

'In my country, the links of fortunes are forged with blood, sweat and tears! Any man nurturing an ambition to become a poet, should first of all store up sufficient fat—like bears and marmots—to allow him to sit on his haunches all winter!'

Morva trembled to her feet, struggling to subdue an emotion that was unfamiliar to her calm, placid nature, a sweeping, fiery sensation that was knotting the muscles in her stomach; causing her knees to shake, making her fingers itch to slap the tanned-hide insensitive cheek of the *grizzly* Canadian.

Her lips had begun forming around an excuse to flee his presence when her grandmother darted a sharp look of warning before proceeding upon a tactless act of betrayal.

'Belvoir, dear boy, it's time the servants were instructed to prepare your rooms. As I expect to be kept busy for the next couple of hours, I suggest you make a tour of the castle grounds. Morva will be pleased to show you around, and to supply all the information you're likely to need.'

'That sounds great to me!' Displaying surprising agility for one of his size, he bounded to his feet and crossed a width of carpet in two giant strides. 'Lead the way, Lady Morva.'

Giving her no time to protest, he gripped her elbow and began forcibly propelling her towards the door. She felt swept by the force of a tornado, her feet barely touching the ground as his ranging stride carried them down a sweep of staircase, across the marbled floor of the Great Hall and out through the main doors, slackening only when a stretch of formal gardens dotted with fountains, stone benches and marble statuary had been left far behind.

She was flushed, wide eyed and panting for breath when he suddenly halted to stare straight ahead, hissing a whistle of appreciation through set teeth.

'That's a mighty impressive set-up!' His admiring gaze travelled slowly along range upon range of greenhouses spun like a huge glass cobweb to trap every available ray of sunshine from dawn until sunset.

'Let's look inside!'

But when he began urging her forward she dug in her heels, making him hesitate just long enough to allow her to comb her scattered wits in search of a plausible explanation.

'There's nothing to see. They're empty . . .'

'Empty? Are you telling me that all that naturally heated space is being allowed to go to waste? Why, for heaven's sake?' His furrowed brow suddenly cleared. 'Have you had trouble with bugs . . . with plant diseases, perhaps?'

Because his oblique criticism of her studious, dreamy father was still rankling, she found it easy to be very angry with the hustling, done-everything, been-everywhere Canadian who had erupted into her quiet pasture with all the finesse of a rampaging bull.

Resenting the need to defend her father's economic measures, she iced.

'There was a time when those greenhouses supplied dozens of house guests with exotic fruits, flowers, and out-of-season vegetables; when the Home Farm was able to meet the needs of kitchen staff demanding daily deliveries of chickens, eggs, milk, cream, butter and cheese. Then, large parties of guests were occupying every bedroom in the castle. Every night tables were laid differently for dinner, sometimes there'd even be a band playing on the lawn. But in those days,' she stressed hardly, 'the castle was staffed by a butler controlling a retinue of footmen, ladies' maids, scullery maids, kitchen maids, housemaids, a cook and a housekeeper. Dozens of servants were also employed in the garden. *Today*, there are only two!'

Unable to trust her voice to remain steady, she cast him one last look of scorn then turned on her heel and ran, ignoring the many lessons in dignity that decreed young ladies must be unfailingly polite; must look cool and serene however much provoked; must behave with dignity and grace throughout every form of crisis.

She slipped inside the castle through a rear entrance

and was just about to sidle past the door of her grandmother's sitting room when it was flung open and an imperious hand beckoned her inside.

'Close the door behind you, my dear.' Her grandmother sounded surprisingly affable. 'Sit down, you and I must have a little chat.' She waited until Morva had obediently perched on the edge of the chair she had indicated. 'You're looking rather pale, my dear, would you like me to order a pot of tea?'

'No, thank you, Granny. I have a slight headache, I was just on my way to my room, intending to lie down for a while.'

'Very sensible my dear. However, that can wait,' her grandmother decreed, displaying scant sympathy, 'there is a very important matter I wish to discuss.'

She sat upright, hands folded neatly in her lap, her frail frame dwarfed by the high, curved back of a capacious leather armchair.

'What opinion have you formed of the new Earl of Howgill?' she surprised Morva.

The question struck her as ludicrous. Dumbly, she withstood her grandmother's probing gaze, wishing she possessed a sufficiently large fund of furious adjectives with which to outline his faults in detail.

'Obviously, the man's a fool!' Her grandmother supplied the answer to her own question. 'Capable of making money, but utterly ignorant of social etiquette, sartorial sense, and of the sort of behaviour expected of a member of the English aristocracy.'

Morva's kind nature rebelled against agreeing with such caustic condemnation, nevertheless, she could not truthfully deny that, cast in the role of a Right Honourable Lord, the Canadian appeared to be a total misfit.

'He has less polish ... less refinement than society will expect of him.' The mild criticism was all her troubled conscience would allow her to utter.

'What a masterly understatement!' her grandmother chuckled. 'However, it is not unknown for gold to purchase honours and even love—or at least a passable imitation. And that, my dear, is where you come in!'

'I ...? Morva felt completely bewildered. 'Whatever do you mean?'

'I've thought of a way of solving all our problems!' Her grandmother leant forward, her cheeks highly flushed, an almost fanatical gleam in her eyes.

'You must marry him, my dear! Once you become Lady Howgill, we will be installed for life in our rightful home. You must leave all the negotiations to me. I promise you, my dear, that when I broach the subject to the new Earl—stressing the benefits to be accrued from a suitable marriage—I will do so with the utmost tact and delicacy. . . .'

CHAPTER THREE

GRANNY must have taken leave of her senses, Morva weakly concluded, feeling fear like the grip of a tightly clenched fist in the pit of her stomach. Listlessly, she began dressing for dinner, depressed by reminders of previous defeats suffered on the very few occasions when she had rebelled against her grandmother's iron will.

But the plan Granny had conceived solely to protect her own interest, to ensure that she remained established for the remainder of her life in what she regarded as her rightful home, was outrageous even when judged by the standards of a Victorian matriarch who had been inculcated from early childhood with the duty to obey rules of tradition laid down to ensure that privileges were maintained—whose own marriage had been arranged purely to protect the continuity of blue blood running through the veins of two noble families.

A glance at the clock sent her hurrying to pick a dress at random from her wardrobe. Family dinners were informal affairs, nevertheless her grandmother was a stickler for punctuality, quick to rebuke anyone who dared to keep her waiting. Hastily she slid a simple brown dress over her head, fumbled with its row of tiny buttons, then rushed to smooth a brush over hair tumbling over her forehead, against flushed cheeks, then down on to her shoulders where it settled in a beech-brown cloud shot with the bronze, gold and reddish tints of autumn. When the clock struck the last of eight chimes she flung down the brush and fled without bothering to pat make-up over cheeks flaunting a march of brown freckles, or to rouge lips gnawed pink, trembling with shy uncertainty.

Her conviction that some phantom hand of destiny was guiding her towards misfortune increased when her eruption into the Great Hall coincided with the arrival of the aggravating Earl. He sauntered out of the library looking slightly bemused, then quickly homed in her direction.

'I've managed to find my way across miles of uncharted territory, yet this place has me foxed. I'm darned if I can find the dining room,' he confessed, casting a rueful glance around many identical doors ranged four square around an expanse of marble floor laid out to resemble an enormous chess board.

'The dining room is this way.' Turning stiffly unforgiving shoulders upon the newly elevated nobleman dressed in a formal grey suit that made him appear almost distinguished, she hurried on ahead, intending to keep two paces in front of his ranging stride, then regretted the impulse when she sensed twin orbs of interest exploring her outline, probing, deliberating, deciding . . . what?

She had been reduced to a blushing quiver of embarrassment by the time she opened the door leading into an ante-room where her grandmother and Percy were waiting.

'Shall we go straight in to dinner?' Her grand-mother's frosty enquiry was accompanied by an imperious wave towards a door leading into the dining room. 'The two men have already been introduced. Fortunately, Percy arrived from London this afternoon just in time to take over the duty of conducting Belvoir over the estate. A duty which you, Morva, had so rudely abandoned!'

Swallowing hard, Morva evaded the mocking glance the Canadian tossed her way as he extended an arm to escort her grandmother into dinner. Meekly, she joined Percy to follow in their wake then gasped, feeling amply revenged when she caught sight of the dinner table.

Either as a mark of respect to the new Earl, or, which was much more likely, in a bid to impress and overawe an unwelcome usurper, her grandmother had obviously supervised the laying of elaborate place-settings. In place of the small circular table they used regularly, a grand oblong table with extra leaves added was groaning under a weight of silver cutlery, crystal glasses, and fragile china. A bewildering array of knives, forks, and spoons—large, small, and medium— were positioned either side of place mats edged with priceless antique lace, and set a little way apart were separate items of cutlery invented so long ago, and for such obscure purposes, that even she was baffled, able to recognise only one peculiarly shaped fork as an implement for spearing pickles.

An almost complete suite of glasses—for water, white wine, red wine and port—were placed diagonally and at a precise distance away from the blades of dinner knives, and mitred linen napkins reared stiff, pointed heads in the direction of candles casting a soft glow over silver candelabra and brilliantly daubed arrangements of fragrant, short-stemmed flowers.

'Belvoir, dear boy, as host, you must take your place at the head of the table,' her grandmother smiled sourly, 'and provided you have no objection, I will occupy the role of your opposite number by sitting at the foot. Morva can sit on your right hand and Percy on mine.'

His hint of hesitation was barely perceptible, the merest suspicion of a pause, the slightest squaring of shoulders before, displaying a quality of cool composure that earned Morva's grudging respect, he embarked upon his first official duty as Earl of Howgill.

But Morva's thrill of triumph quickly turned to shame when, as she sat down opposite Percy, he cast her a glance of amusement which was intercepted by their keen-eyed host. With cheeks flaming, her eyes downcast, she fumbled for a spoon determined to make amends for her family's show of malice by acting as a guide through the intricate maze of cutlery, to lay a trail for the bewildered backwoodsman to follow.

'You made very few comments when we toured the estate, Belvoir.' Percy strove to sound affable as he waited for his soup to be served. 'It's rather impressive, wouldn't you say?'

Carefully, the Earl selected a spoon and tasted his soup before dropping a laconic bombshell into the atmosphere of snobbish condescension.

'It's rather small, run-down, and badly in need of modernisation. Nevertheless, it could be made viable if sufficient time and money were to be invested.'

'Small . . .!' Lady Howgill paused, outraged, with a soup spoon raised halfway to her lips.

'Run-down . . .!' Percy sounded equally incensed. 'The estate cannot be classed as a goldmine, but at least it pays its way!'

The Earl continued eating his soup, looking coolly unrepentant. 'By that, I take it you mean that after having employed men to labour on the land for twelve months of the year you feel amply rewarded by the knowledge that you've broken even. Has no one ever felt an urge to make a profit?'

A seething silence fell while they ate then waited for Buchan, their ancient, slow-moving butler, to remove empty soup plates from the table. Morva chanced to peep from under lowered lashes towards the blunt-speaking stranger who was sipping sherry with evident enjoyment, nodding cool approval of Buchan's choice of white wine to accompany the fish course ascending from the kitchen by way of a hatch being pulleyed by a nervous young man Morva had difficulty in recognising as one of the assistant gardeners, looking patently uncomfortable in his elevated role of footman.

When Buchan began approaching on her right, obviously intending to pour wine into the glass ranged next to her untouched sherry, Morva declined hastily.

'None for me, thank you, Buchan.'

'Oh, but you mustn't refuse, Lady Morva!' When the Earl leant towards her she tried hard not to blink, forced herself to meet eyes spearing contempt through narrowed lids, to watch lips thinning around a dangerously lazy drawl. 'After all, this dinner was planned as a sort of celebration, was it not—or do Border folk still carry out the practice of providing a man with a good dinner before sticking a knife into his back?' When she stared, horrified, he threw back his head and laughed. 'I was merely being facetious, Lady Morva,' he mocked, 'I'm perfectly well aware that the custom was outlawed many centuries ago! Drink your wine, and please try to look less as if you are being forced to feed a wolf who has strayed in from the forest!'

The tinge of shame still lingering in her cheeks deepened. Obviously, he had sized up the situation, read treachery into the plot, and suspected her of collusion. A protesting gasp escaped her lips as she sought for words to deny the implied accusation, but her tongue-tied embarrassment was cut short by her grandmother's haughty voice demanding his attention.

'I do hope, Belvoir, that you were not suggesting earlier that our ancestors had mismanaged your inheritance. Because if you were, I should feel bound to remind you that the Eden family was farming this land decades before the first English settlers transported their energy, knowledge and skills to your homeland—which in those days was no more than an unexplored, uncivilised, uncultivated outpost of the British Empire!'

'Point taken, ma'am.' He disarmed his irate antagonist with a smile so full of charm it left Morva confounded. 'My country is still young, rowdy, and in some places rugged. But unlike the English, its citizens are thirsty for adventure, eager to accept a challenge, reluctant to rest upon their laurels. There are no Everests left to climb, no Amazons to explore, so we manufacture our own. In Alberta, for instance, we've built the longest street in the world, plus a tower that is acknowledged to be the largest free-standing building on earth. But far from being erected as monuments to man's past endeavours they exist to make profit for the businessmen who conceived them—men who are hell-bent on getting where they're going!'

'And do all of you despise tradition when you search after profit?' Morva jerked upright, wondering if she had imagined the slight quiver of fear in her grandmother's voice. 'Do *you* intend disposing of our monuments, smashing the pedestals of honour and glory that have supported Ravenscrag for generations?'

'Continuity need not rule out modern methods or fresh approaches to old situations, Lady Lucy.' Adroitly he sidestepped the question, strengthening Morva's growing conviction that the man they had dubbed a brash backwoodsman was more worldly than he had at first appeared, might even be discovered capable of picking pockets with his tongue!

Her suspicion that the new Earl of Howgill might be laughing up his sleeve grew slowly into a conviction as, while dinner progressed, he proved himself to be more than capable of carving a joint correctly; of exercising the special technique needed for eating artichokes by using his fingers to tear off each leaf in turn before dipping the broad fleshy end into melted butter; and by taking over complete control of the conversation, stating his views on a variety of subjects, inviting comments, yet managing to forestall any move towards the subject of what plans he might have in mind for the future of Ravenscrag.

A desultory silence had fallen by the time Buchan began advancing towards the table to serve port and cheese, a frowning, lip-biting silence which the Earl seemed in no hurry to break as he deliberated over the contents of the cheese board; poured out port for Morva which she did not want, then a measure for himself before passing the decanter along to Percy.

Feeling lightheaded with worry, and with the amount of wine she had been bullied into drinking, Morva twirled the stem of her glass between nervous fingers and cast a covert glance towards the foot of the table, wondering at the depth of thought that had silenced her usually garrulous grandmother.

'You're looking very pale, Lady Morva, is something worrying you?'

She jumped, becoming suddenly conscious of cobalt blue eyes trained steadily as a twin bore shotgun upon a scared rabbit. Desperately aware that this short interval of privacy would probably be the last opportunity she would be given to explain her grandmother's weird eccentricities, she found herself blurting, 'Do you have a grandmother?'

'Unfortunately, no,' he grinned, 'but I do have a very outspoken, dare-devil aunt of eighty-two who bores the pants off anyone who cares to listen to her views about the too-long-delayed emancipation of women and the selfishness of men who supposedly keep them in bondage. Just a couple of weeks before I left home,' he confided dryly, 'she set off on a three-month tour of Europe.'

Morva heaved a heartfelt sigh of relief. Having taken in only half the sense of what he had said, her mind fastened upon the most relevant part of his statement.

'In that case, I've no need to warn you . . . to . . . to explain how difficult and tiresome old ladies can be, how . . .'

'Bossy,' he supplied with a conspiratorial grimace.

'And stubborn,' she nodded, her grave eyes lightening with an appreciative sparkle.

'As well as aggravating, obstreperous, and downright cussed,' he warmed to the theme. 'But also very lovable, don't you agree?'

'Lovable . . .?' Until he frowned, Morva did not realise how quickly her smile must have faded, how her sparkle had been extinguished by a cloud of doubt, a shadow of emotion that could have been fear. 'Oh, yes, of course,' she finally stammered, 'and lovable too.'

'Morva, my dear!' She jerked to attention when her grandmother spoke in an acidly reproving tone that stung a blush of confusion into her cheeks. 'If you've finished eating, would you mind keeping Percy company while I have a private word with Belvoir?'

'Let's stroll together in the garden!' Percy moved with an alacrity that forced Morva to conclude that the entire manoeuvre had been pre-arranged. 'If you would excuse us both, Belvoir?'

The indignation which the Canadian could so easily arouse resurfaced when he acknowledged her brother's request with a nod of dismissal so curt it made her fume. As they walked outside into the garden she read humiliation in Percy's taut profile, saw his hands clench as he fought to come to terms with a reversal of roles that had turned him fom lord into serf, from a popular socialite with great expectations to one of the fringe of hangers-on whose social life was governed by the generosity of sympathetic friends.

It was a warm evening, one of the few balmy nights that descended each summer to surprise the wind-conditioned inhabitants of the Cumbrian Fells, yet as they strolled in silence through the almost day-bright moonlit garden Morva shivered, chilled by the obvious unhappiness of the brother whose merry smile and constant high spirits had made his visits home the highlights of her existence.

'I shall have to find a job.' He halted suddenly at the rim of a fountain, staring as if emotionally attuned to the expression of haughty disdain chiselled into the features of a mighty river god, standing drenched, sad, and covered in lichen, resenting the indignity of one of his rank being reduced to the level of a water fountain. 'I thought I'd have no trouble picking up a couple of directorships,' he confided, slumping with a dejected sigh on to the broad stone rim of the water basin, 'but doors that would have been flung open wide to welcome the Earl of Howgill have been shut in the face of Percy Eden—newly-reduced commoner!'

Quivering with the hurt she was feeling on behalf of her bitterly resentful brother, she sat down next to him and attempted to encourage.

'Something's sure to turn up, Percy, given time.'

'Time is my most quickly advancing enemy,' he refuted brusquely. 'How long do you suppose it will take for friends to forget the misfortune of an heir presumptive whose earldom was snatched from under his nose by a rough-cut, filthy rich Canadian? *Percy who . . .?* they'll be saying in six months' time. *Ah yes, I do vaguely recall the chappie who lost his inheritance— does anyone know what happened to him . . .?*'

'Please, Percy,' she urged shakenly, 'don't allow yourself to become despondent. You'll find a job, I know you will, then you can get married and——'

'How can you be so naive!' he rounded, shocking her silent with the cruel snarl. 'Small wonder Granny has found it impossible—in spite of having stretched her match-making talents to the limit—to arrange a suitable marriage for a granddaughter who is an anachronism in this day and age!'

Morva jumped to her feet, suddenly deathly pale and trembling all over. 'I don't understand!' she appealed in a low, pained whisper.

'Exactly so!' He stood up to glower, a weight of

suppressed anger and resentment forcing cracks to appear in his wall of composure, releasing pressure that escaped in a trickle of words then spurted into a devastating, uncontrollable flood. 'Which chap in his right mind would agree to be joined in matrimony to a girl who knows nothing of life beyond these isolated moors and fells? And make no mistake, Morva, on our level of society marriages don't just happen, they are carefully contrived. Backgrounds, antecedents, even histories of family health are all scrupulously re-searched—at times, when the couple concerned are still in the schoolroom. Love doesn't come into it. Duty to one's family has to be one's main concern. The system is not without its compensations,' he raced on in full, bitter spate, 'for at least when an engagement has to be called off there are no broken hearts on either side. My fiancée and I shook hands after she handed back my ring,' he assured Morva fiercely, 'and I watched her walk away without a qualm. I was of no more use to her, you see—*no point in wasting Daddy's money on a man without a title*!'

'You mean you were prepared to *sell* yourself . . .?' She broke off, her wide eyes mirroring revulsion.

'I was prepared to do my duty, just as you must be,' he responded sharply, stung by a look of distaste he had never expected to see on the face of his adoring young sister. 'If you don't care for the word duty then think of yourself as a debtor! Granny has dedicated the last eighteen years of her life to your upbringing—a duty she did not shirk, even though she had reached an age when most old ladies were expected to tackle nothing more strenuous than needlework. All she asks in return is that you marry Belvoir, so that she may end her days in the castle that has been her home for more than sixty years, ever since the day she became the wife of our grandfather, the eighth Earl of Howgill.'

He shrugged and sauntered a little way away, then cast across his shoulder. 'As for myself, I ask for nothing. For your sake, and for Grandmother's, I was prepared to marry money. Nevertheless, I ask nothing more of any future brother-in-law than that he should offer me a job—preferably a directorship in one of his many U.K. subsidiaries.'

As she stood stock still, shocked and scared by the discovery that a net of family collusion was closing in around her, she struck out towards the one possible escape route which her grandmother had apparently overlooked.

'Did it never occur to either of you that the new Earl might already be married?'

'He isn't.' With one short, terse reply Percy slammed shut the door of freedom. 'Granny always makes certain of such facts before starting negotiations.'

Morva had not moved when Belvoir found her standing in the shadows, as still, cold, and unseeing as the pale marble statuary all around her.

She did not pretend surprise, nor make any effort to resist when, after one quick glance at her stricken features, he took her cold hands between his palms and drew her towards a sandstone bench retaining the warmth of hours of sunshine on its ancient, porous surface.

'I've just had a very interesting discussion with your grandmother, Morva.'

She did not need the familiar form of address to confirm that she had been the object of their discussion, to convince her that in spite of angry, and eventually tearful pleas to her grandmother not to embark upon a course of action she found repugnant, she had proceeded with her attempt to con the new Earl as a rogue car salesman would attempt to con a prospective customer—praising the quality of the merchandise, highlighting its suitability and advantages, camouflaging all flaws and hidden imperfections. . . .

'During dinner, I heard you discussing with my brother the art of trapping,' she murmured bitterly, 'I only hope that when you were taught how to set snares you were also taught how to avoid them!'

If he recognised the hint of warning in her oblique remark he chose to ignore it. Releasing his grip upon her hands he sat back, abandoning her to her misery. Then seconds later, when the scent of tobacco began drifting under her nostrils, she thought how typical he was of rugged outdoor men who chose to become pipe-smokers rather than pose with an exotic cigarette or the even more elegant cheroot.

Her eyes felt fastened to the toes of her shoes, nevertheless, she was conscious of his every movement, heard him puffing at his pipe, caught the small grunt of satisfaction when the tobacco fired, recognised a sigh of satisfaction when he leant back, arms folded across his chest, his long legs stuck way out in front of him.

'I have great plans for Ravenscrag, Morva,' he mused over the top of her downbent head. 'Many successful businesses were founded initially on one man's hunch, on an ability to discover a need that is lacking then filling it.'

She looked up, momentarily distracted from her

troubles by the colossal conceit of the newcomer who apparently imagined that he could make the estate profitable when generations of her ancestors had failed.

'I doubt whether you can have thought of any plan that has not already been tried,' she aswered stiffly, unwilling to be drawn into conversation with a prospective purchaser who might be testing out the wares he had been offered before deciding whether or not to buy. 'We've even tried selling exotic fruit and flowers to Covent Garden. One range of greenhouses was given over entirely to the growing of Muscat grapes, another to rare orchids. Melons, early strawberries, peaches, nectarines and figs all found a ready market, but the project was abandoned when, at the end of the day, it was discovered that the cost of transport was eating too great a hole in the margin of profits.'

She leant back, feeling swallowed by his shadow, when he leant close to encourage.

'But what about the time when large parties of guests were accommodated in the castle?'

She stared, amazed. 'You surely don't imagine that guests—family friends—were expected to pay for hospitality? In any case,' her shoulders lifted in a disdainful shrug, 'Granny is the acknowledged expert on entertaining. There have been no large parties invited to Ravenscrag since my mother . . . departed.'

She felt almost amused by his anxiety to alter the course of their conversation away from what he must have imagined was a painful subject—the departure of her mother from life, rather than her exit from isolation into an endless whirl of social activity.

'I have a mind to revive those house parties.' His

decisive tone captured her startled attention. 'I know of many Canadians, also people of other nationalities, who would jump at the opportunity of spending a vacation in an ancient castle as guests of a genuine English Lord. We could offer them shooting, riding, fishing and sailing, picnic lunches and dinner parties, a taste, in fact, of the sort of living that was enjoyed by aristocratic families during what they would no doubt have termed "the good old days".'

'But could you afford to entertain on such a grand scale?' she gasped, her mind whirling. 'The cost of employing sufficient staff to look after your guests would be enormous!'

'Not if guests were prepared to pay for their bout of self-indulgence.'

He leant back to puff at his pipe, smiling with the air of a businessman well satisfied with the results forecast by his computer mind.

'There is just one drawback to my plan which must be resolved before I start putting the wheels in motion,' he continued assaulting her shocked ears. 'Folk who flock across the Atlantic in a nostalgic search for family roots are prepared to spend generously, nevertheless the majority are tough cookies who demand value for money. Consequently, when our first guests arrive, expecting to be greeted by a peer of the realm, they'll hardly be impressed by the discovery that their host is as much a stranger to the aristocratic way of life as they are themselves.'

Swiftly, taking her completely by surprise, he reached out a hand to cup her small pointed chin within a huge palm.

'I'm a member of the club, Morva, but I don't know the rules!' he appealed in a rough-gentle voice that brought back to mind the descriptions she had read of smooth-running rivers concealing turbulent rapids; snow-muffled peaks nurturing the needle-sharp rims of hidden glaciers; green carpets of spruce and aspen flowing across floors of valleys lined with sheer rock walls; fierce-horned sheep that were shy of people and huge, lumbering bears with a taste for honey. . . .

'I am accustomed to living in a society whose customs are simple and flexible,' he sounded almost coaxing, 'consequently, I have need of a helpmate, someone capable of guiding me through the intricacies of protocol, ceremony, and centuries-old conventions, a hostess who can arrange dinner parties, and control and instruct servants. In short, Morva, I need a wife who can carry out the sort of role for which, according to your grandmother, you have been trained since childhood.'

She felt stunned, cornered as prey conscious of being stalked then clashing head-on with a pursuer who had somehow managed to change direction.

With defeat staring her in the face—defeat in the shape of a grandmother demanding her pound of flesh; a brother who had pinned his last hopes upon her reacting to the call of duty, and a hard-headed businessman who had somehow been persuaded that the purchase of a suitable bride was a sound financial investment—she rose to her feet, tensing her slim body to the rigidity of a lance in an attempt to conceal violent inner trembling.

'Could a position be found for my brother Percy in the proposed . . . merger?' she husked, calling upon centuries of inbred dignity.

'Certainly,' he confirmed, rising to douse her courage with his tall shadow, 'I have a job in mind that is exactly suited to your brother's . . . er, shall we say, traditional talents?'

His mild sneer sparked a flicker of spirit into her blank, unreadable eyes.

'Aren't you being rather hypocritical, Lord Howgill,' she accused coldly. 'My brother may have a fundamental dislike of taking orders, may have been raised to believe in the hereditary principle, but then, presumably, so have you. For how else can you explain the similarities existing between yourself and your great-grandfather who, by your own admission, spent more time over the choice of a suit than he did upon soliciting a bride!'

CHAPTER FOUR

'TIME,' Belvoir had impressed upon the press-ganged, blue-blooded employees of his newly formed company, 'is fast becoming one of the most valuable commodities on earth! Consequently, I must insist that each one of you should account to me personally for every second that is wasted while we're getting our new enterprise off the ground.'

Not surprisingly, Lady Howgill's proposal that the betrothed couple should decide upon a decently prolonged engagement had received an immediate veto from their ruthless chairman.

'Long periods of waiting, of whatever kind, are always irksome.'

Lady Howgill had bridled. 'It was customary in my young days for engaged couples to be given an opportunity of getting to know each other well before setting a date for the wedding!' she had argued, tossing an icy glance in the direction of her totally uninterested granddaughter. 'Also, there is a certain amount of excitement about an engagement which is after all supposed to be a period of courtship, of intimate dinners and outings with her fiancé that a prospective bride must be allowed to enjoy if she is not to feel cheated.'

'An engagement can also be classed as a probationary period during which either party is entitled to express a change of heart or of mind!' Belvoir had reminded with a hint of warning that had effectively killed the argument stone dead. 'The wedding will take place just as soon as all the formalities have been completed,' he had proceeded to bury the subject without hope of resurrection. 'A brief, informal ceremony will be held in the family chapel, with as few guests and as little publicity as can reasonably be managed.'

But on one issue at least Lady Howgill had remained adamant, Morva reflected in the privacy of her room, dragging sad eyes away from a vista of moorland and hills changing appearance from sunny to sombre at the caprice of sun-darting rays through slowly closing ranks of grey cloud. She turned to glance at the object representing her grandmother's one and only victory over the new Earl who in the space of a couple of weeks had gradually withdrawn a velvet glove from a fist of iron.

'Morva will be married in a *proper* wedding dress,' her grandmother had insisted with a tremble of extreme agitation. 'She will walk down the aisle accompanied by bridal attendants and make her vows before a congregation made up, if not of friends and relatives, then at least of estate workers and their families whose love and respect she has been privileged to enjoy since childhood!'

A hint of mirthless amusement curled Morva's lips as she mused upon the probable reaction of the Earl when confronted by a bride wearing the *proper* sort of dress her grandmother had in mind—the dress she had worn herself on her wedding day but which she had diplomatically omitted to mention had been bequeathed to her by her mother—a dedicated follower of fashions set by a much-loved princess from over the sea who, upon the death of her formidable mother-in-law, Queen Victoria, had reigned with her husband over Edwardian England.

A tap upon the door distracted her attention away from the dress which only days previously had been unearthed from the cedarwood chest where for decades it had been preserved within a bag of fine white muslin. She was just about to call out permission to enter when her decision was pre-empted by the appearance of her grandmother stepping over the threshold.

'Good heavens, girl, haven't you even begun dressing yet? I said you should have a maid to help you!'

'Please, Granny, don't start that argument all over again, I'm all but ready—I merely have to slip the dress over my head.'

Stifling a regretful sigh, Morva abandoned all hope of further privacy and rose to her feet, tightening the belt of her dressing gown as if girding a suit of protective armour around the body of a novice preparing for a first sortie into battle. Warily, she eyed her grandmother, noting that she was already attired for the ceremony in finery that had been unearthed from the same cedarwood chest that had held her wedding gown—in a dress with a bodice and basque of stiff grey satin and a cape of accordion-pleated grenadine. A toque of pale mauve velvet completed the outfit, a dainty hat designed to flatter the high-piled coiffures that had stamped the hallmark of elegance upon indulged, fashion-conscious ladies of Edwardian society.

'I must say it is a relief to know that there will be no relatives or friends attending the wedding,' her grandmother sniffed as she sat down, carefully spreading her skirts around her. 'I could not have borne the embarrassment of having to explain in person that your wedding day has had to be fitted into a very tight schedule because our home is to be turned into a hotel which the new Earl is determined to have ready to accommodate its first influx of paying guests for the start of the shooting season. The Glorious Twelfth!' delicately she shuddered, 'what a day of ignominy that will be for all of us. Thank goodness your dear father has been spared the agony of being trampled by the march of commercialism into the ancestral home!'

'It's too late for regrets, Granny.' Morva slid out of her dressing gown and reached towards the wedding dress hanging against a wall in a shadowy corner looking rather as she was feeling—like a headless ghost, a remote spirit suspended in mid air, being seen to move, to speak and otherwise exist, yet having no real entity. 'We have both been thoroughly briefed and have agreed to carry out the duties apportioned to us. In my capacity of head housekeeper—which carries with it the title of Countess Howgill—I shall be responsible for controlling all the guest accommodation; for the interviewing, training and supervision of staff; for checking supplies, and for such things as adding finishing touches in the way of flowers, fruit and chocolates to the rooms of new arrivals. In short, to copy exactly the routine of previous Countesses of Howgill. How wise of you to have insisted upon teaching me such duties even though, at the time, there seemed not the remotest possibility of my ever being called upon to exercise such skills. As the chores you have been allocated are far from onerous, perhaps,' she paused to consider thoughtfully, 'we should be feeling gratitude instead of resentment towards the man whose high-powered business methods have left us breathless—yet permanently installed in our ancestral rut.'

'Grateful!' Her grandmother gave an unladylike snort. 'If I had suspected for one moment that a man of such wealth, one whose business commitments leave him very little time to spare, would insist upon going to such drastic lengths in order to make Ravenscrag pay its way, I would not have dreamt of approaching him——' She broke off, then with a flustered glance at her watch hurriedly decided.

'However, plans are already too far advanced for change, we must try to make the best of an impossible situation. I shall keep my part of our bargain by searching for details of ancient customs that have been allowed to fall into disuse, and by hunting out recipes for local delicacies that might help to enliven the jaded palates of rich social climbers. Beyond that, I shall do nothing but retire to my rooms and remain there for as long as our home is allowed to be overrun by noisy, demanding intruders intent upon aping their betters!'

She rose to her feet, drawing her elegant frame erect.

'As you insist upon coping alone, I shall leave you to finish dressing. I suggest you make haste,' she warned dryly, stepping towards the door, 'I cannot imagine your progressive-minded bridegroom being impressed with the excuse that it is customary for a bride to arrive late for her wedding.'

She hesitated with her hand on the door knob, the slight rise of colour in her cheeks causing Morva to brace in readiness for the spate of marital wisdom usually directed towards a young, nervous bride on her wedding day. But it soon became apparent that prudish embarrassment would cause her grandmother to offer no more than a delicate observation.

'A wife is expected to humour her husband's taste as much as possible, my dear. If she loves him, this can give her pleasure, however, if whims and impositions should be imposed which diminish her happiness in some respect, she is under no moral obligation to submit.' She fumbled with the door, then as if forced by conscience to console a bride looking completely bewildered, she added a stern postscript.

'I have often suspected that you have been far more influenced by your choice of reading matter than by the realities of everyday life, Morva, my dear. Love and romance are idealised in fiction; in marriage, however, consideration and companionship are much to be preferred.'

Morva was still pondering over the prim, old-fashioned tone of her grandmother's lecture when a glance at the clock told her that Percy would soon be arriving to escort her to the church.

Hastily, she slipped over her head a plain satin underskirt which time had tinted until it shone oyster-white through a delicate overdress of mousseline de soie, a deliciously soft material that lifted and fell on the slightest breeze, giving to the full skirt edged with three tiers of finely pleated frills a charming fullness in spite of its light, almost floating reaction to her slightest movement. The bodice drew folded bands of the soft material around gently curving breasts then crossed where they met to span a waist mercifully slender enough to have no need of the stays stiffened with whalebone and threaded with laces which at first sight she had dubbed an instrument of female torture.

Mechanically, she stepped in front of a full-length mirror then quickly drew away, almost scared by the effect the dress had had upon her reflection, her senses reeling from the impact of seeing her own sudden blossoming from plain brown obscurity into an exquisitely gilded lily—slender-stemmed neck and elegant head rising from a cloud of oyster-white petals.

Trembling slightly she brushed aside the bridal veil she had flatly refused to wear and almost collapsed on to a stool in front of her dressing table, willing her fingers not to shake as she arranged an ornament into her sternly confined coiffure—white lace wings, one pinned each side of a beech-brown chignon threaded through with a rope of family pearls. White elbow-length gloves completed a toilette that left her transformed, so much so that Percy, after tapping on the door and responding to her call to enter, stood rooted, his shocked eyes roving over the lovely, demure young bride who could conceivably have stepped out from behind the frame of an ancestral portrait.

He advanced slowly towards her. 'I feel I am looking through a keyhole into an age long past, an age of innocence, chivalry, and sweet harmless pleasures!'

It would have been impossible for her not to have felt flattered by this confirmation that she had never looked better on a day when her confidence most needed a boost, the day of her marriage to a man whose attitude towards herself was kind, even indulgent, but whose friendliness towards the rest of her family had seemed to vanish overnight—the night she had been forced into accepting a proposal couched more along the lines of a business contract, a formal agreement to supply certain articles for a settled price, the articles in question being a home for her grandmother and a job for Percy; the price, marriage to a man who in the manner of his great grandfather had assessed the benefits of matrimony, then with cool, businesslike precision had proposed to the most suitable female in his vicinity!

'What I find puzzling,' Percy frowned, his thoughts obviously attuned to her own, 'is why Belvoir so quickly succumbed to Granny's persuasion. Oh, I know that once, in the heat of the moment, I accused you of being unmarriageable,' he responded apologetically to her pained blush, 'but that wasn't strictly true. All infants grow up eventually, some just take longer than others to reach maturity. However, rugged good looks and unlimited wealth add up to an extremely eligible bachelor! With all he has going for him, Belvoir could have taken his pick of society beauties, so why has he chosen to marry a girl who, though sweet and very lovable, is an utter simpleton so far as a man's physical needs are concerned? You *do* realise what will be expected of you, Morva . . .?' he questioned keenly, eyeing the blush of mortification running wild in her cheeks.

'Of course I do!' In spite of a heart that felt lifted on the wings of agitated butterflies, she managed to answer calmly. 'I may have led a sheltered life, but I have had access to newspapers and magazines containing articles aimed at supplying explicit details about every aspect of sexual behaviour to simpletons such as myself who may be in need of guidance.'

'Oh, excellent . . .!' For the first time in his life her brother seemed at a loss for words.

'Naturally,' she continued with a brave show of composure, 'The tenth Earl of Howgill will be looking to his wife to provide him with an heir. But his most immediate requirement is for a figurehead. As you know, lots of businesses buy titles because they look good on printed letterheads; he is simply following this procedure by cashing in on his newly gained title and investing money in a wife who possesses the background, breeding and social graces that he lacks. I honestly believe,' she confided confidently, 'that success in business is his all-consuming passion; that there isn't the faintest streak of romanticism in his nature.'

'You think so . . .?' Percy looked doubtful.

'I do,' she nodded, turning aside to pick up an ivory-backed prayer book. 'Because if he could spare the time to fall in love, why on earth would he be marrying me?'

Her air of bravado was quite easily maintained while Percy escorted her downstairs, past the crowd of excited servants who had gathered in the hall, then along a path wending through the castle grounds towards a small private chapel. But the moment she stepped inside the porch and caught sight of the two angelically dressed children who were to be her only bridal attendants her knees threatened to buckle, causing her to clutch her brother's arm in a grip of nervous trepidation that tightened to panic when the hush that had fallen inside the chapel was broken by an organist's triumphant rendering of the Wedding March.

The aisle leading up to the altar rails was no more than a few yards long, yet she felt she had dragged leaden feet past a mile of pews crammed with smiling faces before she faltered to a standstill and was handed into the keeping of a tall, broad stranger with an expression as grave and unfamiliar as his formal suit and with a handclasp that was frightening in its strength yet which imposed an indefinable sense of comfort when it gripped.

She met his glance then quickly looked away from cobalt blue eyes blazing what might have been the look of a man of today condemning an ingenuous bride of yesterday.

Then the conventional ritual began with an introductory sermon delivered on the meaning and purpose of marriage.

'. . . to give to each other mutual society, help and comfort . . . to know each other in love, united in body, heart and life . . . to beget children. . . .'

Standing demurely, with eyes downcast, Morva mentally added her own additional reasons to the list.

. . . to provide Granny with a permanent home . . . and a well-paid directorship for Percy. . . .

She was too numb to respond other than with a slight shake of her head to the sternly voiced question directed towards the bride and bridegroom.

'Is there any reason why this marriage should not take place?'

Then in no time at all, or so it seemed, Percy responded to the cue: 'Who giveth this woman . . .?', by taking her right hand and passing it palm downward to the clergyman before retiring into the background leaving her feeling that she was no more than a family heirloom that had been regretfully auctioned off to the highest bidder—a bridegroom who recited his vows in a slow drawl and made no attempt to place a kiss of ownership upon the lips of his latest possession when the marriage ceremony was concluded with the traditional words of warning.

'Those whom God hath joined together let no man put asunder!'

'*Morva, my dear, you made a radiant bride!*' Incredibly, as they stood outside the church waiting to accept the congratulations and good wishes of the small gathering of estate workers, her grandmother began dabbing at her eyes with a dainty lace handkerchief. 'And you, Belvoir,' she acknowledged on a positively insulting note of surprise, her eyes scouring his suit down to the last perfectly placed button, 'are looking very handsome; positively presentable!'

The slow, easy grin that had captured Morva's attention at their very first meeting was momentarily resurrected by her grandmother's uncharacteristic lack of diplomacy.

'Know first who you are then dress accordingly,' he teased, tightening his loose clasp around Morva's wrist. She looked up, responding instinctively to her husband's first command and saw a strange expression cross his features as his eye mused over her white-winged head, across flushed cheeks, then down to where a pulse was beating a puzzling, new, yet strangely exciting rhythm in the childish hollow at the base of her throat.

But the thoughts crossing his mind could not have been pleasant, for his tone was impatient—verging upon curt—when he turned cool blue eyes upon her grandmother.

'Well, Lady Lucy, you've had your fun, the charade you insisted upon has been played out, so perhaps now you will excuse me while I change into comfortable gear and get down to some work.'

'Work!' Morva's own scandalised reaction found an

echo in her grandmother's voice. 'But Belvoir, dear boy, this *is* your wedding day—and Morva's too,' she tacked on as an afterthought. 'Whatever the reasons motivating a marriage—and I would be the first to admit that for centuries, to the aristocracy it has been simply a matter of bargain and sale with affection and natural inclination coming very far down the list—it is most important that appearances be maintained.'

'Please, Granny,' Morva appealed, raising a hand to her hot cheeks, 'you make me sound like a piece of merchandise to be made the most of in the marriage market!'

As swiftly as she had done many times in the past, her grandmother squashed this hint of rebellion.

'Might I suggest, my dear,' the look she speared was far from genial, 'that instead of indulging your taste for romantic poetry, you dip into the family archives for a dose of historical truth! Chronicles penned long before the invention of the printing press will soon convince you that the days of so-called chivalry were greatly overrated, that marriage making was a regular trade amongst the highest ranks, and that even reigning monarchs had no scruples whatsoever about making huge profits by encouraging knight to bid against knight for a licence to marry well.'

Morva's hold on her prayer book tightened as she stood with head bowed, feeling shrivelled by the contempt her bridegroom was making no attempt to conceal. But then humiliation was replaced by shocked surprise when his steadying grip descended upon her waist, pulling her close against a frame that felt powerful as a bulwark, as comforting as his relaxed, teasing drawl.

'If that's the case, then I guess I've found myself a

bargain!' The pressure of his fingers made a heavy contrast to his lightly tossed words. 'My country cannot lay claim to centuries of honourable tradition, nevertheless, it has become customary among business tycoons to celebrate the closing of a deal with a good meal. So I guess work will have to wait a little while longer,' Morva's heart lurched when he hooked her hand within the crook of his elbow and treated her to a wide grin. 'Let me take you to lunch, bargain bride, so that we may drink a toast to the signing of a contract which I hope will turn out to be mutually beneficial.'

A buffet lunch for estate workers had been set out in a barn especially decorated for the occasion, but a separate and beautifully appointed table had been laid for four in Granny's small sitting room. Yet in spite of hours of effort by the servants, in spite of her grandmother's determined cheerfulness and the light-hearted banter that had obviously been rehearsed by Percy for the special occasion, she sensed the luncheon falling flat while as course followed course, her bridegroom's earlier promise of conviviality failed to materialise.

When finally he threw down his napkin and rose to his feet she felt his polite request to be excused as a personal slight, an indication that the prospect of spending hours in the company of his new bride could in no way compete with the more stimulating demands of business.

'Knowing how much you look forward to a daily gallop with Clio, I guess you won't be too upset if I spend the next few hours attempting to restore order out of the chaos of correspondence littering my desk,' he addressd her without a hint of apology.

'Just one minute, Belvoir!' Percy intervened just as his host was about to take his leave. 'As I have a long-standing engagement to attend a "thrash" this evening, I intend leaving for London almost immediately!'

The enquiring lift of the Earl's eyebrows, his deliberately maintained silence, had the effect of turning Percy's rather pale complexion brick red.

'. . . It's just that, no reference has yet been made to the position I am to be offered on the board of one of your companies, so naturally, I've been wondering. . . .'

Morva raised her eyes from the plate she had been studying to direct an indignant glare, daring her husband to prolong his victim's misery. She caught a flash of amusement in his returned stare—the sort of look a bear might bestow upon a belligerent rabbit—then hurriedly resumed her interest in her ornately patterned plate when he responded to her dumb entreaty.

'Never in my life have I reneged on a promise, Eden. Nor am I ever likely to forget about the job you demanded in exchange for your sister!' Morva sensed that his eyes were still upon her, so he could not have missed her mortified wince. Nevertheless, he proceeded to escalate her lukewarm dislike into a passion very near to hatred. 'However, as there is no directorship vacant at present, the only upwardly mobile spot I am able to offer is that of personal assistant to the chairman of the newly formed Howgill Holidays Inc, based permanently in Cumbria, and carrying a salary which, though initially modest, will be reviewed after a probationary period and adjusted according to merit!'

For the following hours, from noon to early nightfall, Morva rode Clio across moorland and fells, blind to shadow-cast dips and hollows, to hoof-panicked sheep, decapitated wild flowers, the indignant flight of game birds from roosts among the heather, and to gaping grey sores gouged by mechanical monsters in softly rounded hills nurturing hearts of granite.

Struck by a metaphorical comparison with the man who wore relaxed informality as a casing for a knife-sharp brain, she pulled on the reins, drawing Clio to a halt in order to dwell without distraction upon the deceitful Canadian who had ambled into their lives like an amiable bear, then immediately turned grizzly upon learning that he would be required to work if he wished to add to his already ample store of honey.

I never renege on a promise! he had reminded Percy.

The very last thing she sought was a share in his worldly goods, yet just a few hours previously she had felt so comforted, so foolishly deceived by his promise to love and cherish. . . . Obviously the man lacked integrity. Obviously he had only once spoken the truth—when he had enlisted her sympathy by confessing ignorance of the rules of the ancient, honourable club to which chance had admitted him as a member. *'I have need of a helpmate, a guide. . . .'*

Without doubt, he needed someone to demonstrate the ideal of fighting weakness in order to preserve honour!

Clio jerked into motion, made suddenly conscious of the existence of spurs attached to the boots of her rider.

'Giddup, Clio!' She heard the strangely sharp

command. 'There's a grizzly bear in urgent need of training!'

There was no one in sight when Morva entered the castle, no one to comment upon her absence from dinner, or to delay her race up many flights of stairs to the attic where her wedding dress had been stored. For frantic moments she rummaged inside cedarwood chests before pouncing upon the article she had been seeking, then without a backward glance at debris littering the floor she hurried back downstairs carrying a bundle under her arm, then forced herself to walk along the tapestry-hung gallery giving access to the suite of rooms traditionally reserved for the Earl and Countess of Howgill.

Her heart sank, as it usually did whenever she stepped inside the imposing suite. Familiarity had not managed to breed indifference to the magnificence of a centre bedroom covered from dado to cornice with dark red Chinese silk that had been transported, together with the rest of the furnishings, by way of caravans of camels and yaks, for thousands of miles through deserts and across mountains towards a Mediterranean port from which the cargo had been shipped by an earlier Earl with the intention of transforming his Cumberland Castle into an Oriental palace.

Paying mental tribute to whichever destiny had decided that the Earl's fortunes should wane long before his enthusiasm, she scurried into the bathroom, averting her eyes from sets of bronze chung-bells; ornaments of jade said to be vested with mystical meaning; animal claws, horns, tails and gaping jaws carved upon the surface of ancient wine vessels; paintings done on silk depicting Oriental maidens reclining amid falling cherry blossoms, and exotic cats coiled into serpentine poses casting glares of pure red garnet upon dragons and leopards, hawks and tigers crouched around the edges of a canopy drawing a passion-red screen of silk—billowing noiseless as a breath—around what custom had decreed should be the nuptial bed of every Earl and Countess of Howgill.

After leaving the bathroom she laid shivering for what seemed hours between scented sheets—a dutiful bride covered from neck to toe in a nightdress of finest lawn, with a pintucked bodice and frills of lace around collar, wristbands and hem, and with a matching mobcap perched upon hair parted primly in the middle of her forehead then left to fall around her shoulders in a burnished, beech-brown cloud.

Every nerve in her body responded with a jerk to the sound of a door opening and closing with a dull thud. Through the closed film of curtain she glimpsed a man's outline; heard the creak of a chair when he sat down, followed by a couple of thumps as he discarded his shoes.

It was only when he moved out of earshot towards the bathroom that she realised that for the past tense minutes she had barely drawn breath. She sank back against the pillows, white faced and trembling, just dimly beginning to realise how mentally ill-equipped, how physically immature, she must appear to her free-thinking, free-spirited, madly progressive bridegroom.

She had just begun sidling from between the sheets, her mind too intent upon escape to register the padding of approaching footsteps, when the bed curtain was impatiently ripped aside and she was suddenly confronted by her startled, stark-naked husband.

'What the hell . . .!'

Scarlet with confusion she jerked aside, turning her back upon a bronzed muscular body which even her inexperienced eyes had labelled magnificent.

'Why are you here, Morva?' The sharp question razed past her fiery earlobe. 'And why are you dressed like a sacrificial kid awaiting slaughter?'

She forced her limbs to move, willed her eyelids to lift, and was relieved to see him tying the belt of a towelled robe.

'We made a bargain,' she swallowed hard. '*I* was not speaking lightly when I promised to keep my word.'

'Ah, now I get the picture! The virgin wife is willing to endure the ultimate sacrifice in order to set an example of integrity to a husband without conscience!'

Looking intolerably goaded, he thrust clenched fists into the pockets of his robe and swung on his heel as if unable to endure the sight of a profile etched ghostly pale against an exotic red background.

'Thank you, but no thank you, Morva,' he declined hatefully. 'You are welcome to my bed but not to my company. I'll sleep next door in the dressing room.'

'Why . . .?' she gasped through a throat aching with mortified tears.

'Because *I* shall decide when my wife is to be bedded—and that will not happen until I've judged her to be good and ready, when I feel certain that she has revised her quaint notion that it is acceptable for a girl to be bred solely to provide a pay cheque for layabout members of her family! I can't even hazard a guess how long it will take to drag you out of the nineteenth century,' he swung round to glare condemnation of her deliberately chosen night attire. 'But one thing I swear—you will remain a virgin wife until the day you cast off your hair shirt and voluntarily concede that the past is a bucket of ashes!'

CHAPTER FIVE

FOR several weeks convoys of builder's lorries had been transporting men and materials across bleak moorland roads, invading the privacy of the furred and feathered inhabitants of the no-man's land of peace and tranquillity which the hustling, decisive, deaf-to-all excuses Earl was determined to see entered as a 'must' in all top-market tourist brochures.

Morva frowned at heaps of builder's rubble strewn around the courtyard, sympathising with her Granny's resentment of the upset that had forced her to retreat, vowing never to set foot outside her personal suite of rooms until the last nail had been hammered, the last power drill silenced. She sighed, disliking the contrast made by modern pipework running adjacent to ancient lead gutters and downspouts blending harmoniously into weathered stone.

'Tourists are a race of contradictory creatures,' a voice mocked from behind her shoulder, 'entranced by the idea of water having to be drawn from wells, yet insisting that an unlimited amount of showers and hot baths is essential to their comfort.'

Slowly she turned to face the man whose proven ability to read her thoughts was uncanny, having to remind herself yet again that the Earl dressed in cowboy garb of brightly checked shirt and coarse blue denims really was her husband.

'As are modern-day Croesus,' she completed the analogy, 'who are able to spend freely, unhampered by

71

the dread of a mounting overdraft, yet who obviously enjoy the rush and hassle of big business. In common with most people of average means, I used to envy the wealthy their freedom to buy whatever they fancy without even bothering to ask the price. But lately, I've been wondering . . .' she hesitated, seeking words that would not sound censorious or disapproving.

'Go on,' he prompted, eyeing her keenly, 'you have been wondering what?'

'Whether I should like to become permanently chained to a treadmill,' she finished simply 'whether unlimited wealth really can compensate for having to work so hard at staying rich.'

'Some see a man's work as a self-portrait.' His grin seemed tinged with wry humour. 'In which case, you would no doubt picture me as a King Midas, a fool who attracted pity rather than envy when even his food turned to gold the moment he touched it.' Negligently, he reached out to clasp a hand around her waist, drawing her stiffly unresponsive body into his arms.

'I can think of no greater penance to impose upon a man than the frustration of feeling his bride turning cold at his touch, sensing her frigid absence of warmth, facing the daunting prospect of trying to make love to a petrified madonna offering an unyielding body and cold lips to her husband. A man could soon become discouraged by such a passionless paragon, Morva. . . .'

As his dark head lowered she felt his warm breath brushing across her softly parted lips, then in a sudden burst of frustration he pulled her close, crushing her mouth beneath his with a surging, demanding, irresistible force that caught her unprepared, caused her to clutch at arms holding her steady as a rock while she was swept, buffeted, then finally submerged to the point of drowning in a torrent of racing emotions. Desperately she clung to the one solid object remaining in a world turned topsy turvy, sliding her palms along taut biceps, across a breadth of powerful shoulders, then entwining frantic fingers behind a neck that felt immovable as a tree trunk that could be bent but never broken.

Expertly, he probed the tender curve of her mouth, his lips creating chaos wherever they touched, sparking nerves into vibrant life, tearing aside the veil of innocence that had hidden terrifying yearnings and wicked impulses she had not known she possessed, causing her to forget that ever since their disastrous wedding night he had barely acknowledged her existence, that he had left her to sleep alone in his bed with tortured thoughts and tormented dreams dominated by one swift glimpse of a tanned, magnificently proportioned body and by the intolerable hurt and sense of rejection she had suffered since the moment he had walked away. . . .

'Oh, there you are, Belvoir!'

Without a word of apology for his untimely intrusion, Percy strode into the courtyard. Morva jerked back to reality, her cheeks scarlet with embarrassment as she tried to pull out of the shocking embrace. But Troy held her captive, locking both hands around her waist, reminding her with a look that they were man and wife and that the true state of their marital affairs was to be kept secret even from members of her family. 'Well, now that you've found me, state your business and get back to work!' Troy growled, without bothering to turn his head.

The curt dismissal drove a tinge of colour into Percy's cheeks. Foolishly, he allowed antagonism to creep into his tone.

'Your decision to advertise Ravenscrag as a centre for conferences, product launches, and business dinners appears to be bearing fruit. I've just had to turn down a booking proposed on behalf of a company in search of accommodation, opportunity for a few hours' relaxation, and a reception and dinner for one hundred of their overseas representatives.'

'You've done what!'

Percy blanched when twin spears of cobalt blue were aimed towards him.

'I've turned the booking down,' he defied valiantly, 'we're not due to open for another month and the company concerned requires accommodation in two weeks' time.'

'No hotel can afford to turn down a booking that size, especially when its main aim is to build up a reputation for first-class service and close attention to the needs of its clientele!'

'You're being very unreasonable, Troy!' With an angry jerk Morva escaped his clutches and retreated a couple of feet away. 'You are perfectly well aware that there aren't enough rooms ready yet! And even if there were, considering the small number of staff at present employed we could not possibly cope with one hundred guests for dinner.'

'Oh, yes we can, and what's more we will!' He snapped a directive to Percy. 'Get right back on to the company concerned and tell them that we will be pleased to accommodate members of their staff during the period quoted. Explain the circumstances existing at present, and apologise in advance for any slight inconveniences that may arise, while at the same time stressing that these will be kept to an absolute minimum.'

'Meanwhile,' the eyes he turned upon Morva were as impersonal as the computer he referred to constantly in his search for answers to rapidly punched problems, 'you come with me. Once we've made a tour of the castle and decided which rooms can most quickly be made ready for occupation, you can get cracking with the next most important job of employing extra staff.'

'Cook will be furious when an order demanding dinner for one hundred guests is dropped into her lap,' she hedged uncertainly, then was galvanised into action by his brusque ultimatum.

'If she has any doubts about her ability to cope she will have to go! Cooking one hundred dinners is not such a big deal, for years my aunt catered for the same number of hungry cowboys, providing two hefty meals a day with less than half a dozen helpers in the cook house!'

'Our cook, Mrs Mackay, is no hash slinger,' Percy patronised with a smile that set Morva's teeth on edge. 'On the contrary, she is extremely proud of the *Grand Diploma* she gained from *Le Cordon Bleu de Paris* which she has often assured me can be classed as a passport into the finest kitchens of the world. It's a mystery why she has remained with us for so long. One probable reason,' he sniffed, 'could be that she regards herself as one of the family.'

'Good!' Troy quickly retaliated. 'I'm delighted to learn that we have a master chef employed on the premises. As that is the case, Morva,' he instructed, keeping his eyes trained upon Percy's haughty features, 'I suggest you sweeten Cook's sour reaction with the news that we have decided to double her salary. I've found there's no limit to the things people will do for an extra couple of shekels, haven't you, Eden?' he taunted. 'Even cupid, the naked cherub, has had to be provided at times with a money pouch!'

Morva stared, shocked by the antagonism existing between her deposed brother and the tough Canadian who seemed to delight in cracking the whip of authority over his head. She shuddered with self-revulsion, ashamed of the traitorous responses aroused by the husband who had demanded her betrayal of life-held principles; the denouncement of ancient, honourable tradition in exchange for the favour of becoming his true wife!

A wave of tribal loyalty overwhelmed her when the usurper dared to dismiss her patrician brother with an abrupt threat.

'Get moving, Eden, you know what you have to do! And in case your gentlemanly upbringing should rule that practising the art of commerce is beneath your dignity, I want to make one thing very clear—if you mess up this deal, I'll nail you!'

Tight-lipped with indignation, Morva submitted to being hustled through the East Entrance and into a kitchen in the process of being gutted of ancient black-leaded ranges; past larders lined with meat safes and dark recesses choked with lumber, then through the Painted Hall towards a staircase flanked by a larger-than-life statue of a winged and naked Mercury.

She ought not to have been confounded by his lack of delicacy and good taste when he stopped to study the statue of the winged messenger, his frozen flight unimpeded by even a vestige of clothing.

'Did you know that at the beginning of each fig harvest it is customary for the first fig picked from a tree to be devoted to Mercury?' he grinned, cocking a wicked eyebrow. 'A sense of fellow-feeling assures me that he could make much better use of the fig leaves!'

Colour rioted in her cheeks at this indelicate reference to the night she had surprised him naked, yet rendered immune to embarrassment by his ultra-thick hide.

'Mercury, the god of science and commerce!' He leant across the banister to pat a bare marble rump. 'His presence here in Ravenscrag could be considered a good omen, don't you think?'

'A very apt symbol,' she agreed on a tremor of indignation, 'considering that he is also the patron of rogues, vagabonds and thieves!'

He tossed back his head and laughed aloud, then surprised her by revealing a knowledge of literature that struck her as entirely contradictory to the twin roles of hard-headed businessman and earthy cowboy which he played so convincingly.

'So you think me a "snapper-up of unconsidered trifles", eh, Morva?' He bent his dark head to tease. 'But surely, by implication, you are undervaluing your own worth?'

They had reached the head of a polished oak staircase lined with a profusion of barley sugar bannisters by the time she had gathered sufficient composure to take up the thread of his teasing words. She stopped dead in her tracks, then bolstered by the presence of ancestral portraits ranged with lofty superiority around oak panelled walls, she spun round to condemn quietly.

'Must you be so hard on my brother? After all, his

loss was your gain—you now own everything he was brought up to regard as his inheritance!'

'Then he should thank me for doing him a favour.' The even tenor of his reply sounded dangerously akin to the low rumbling of a geyser building up pressure to spout. 'Suddenly he has been forced to join the human race, given an opportunity to earn his own medals on the corporate battlefield, to rise to the top through his own initiative by devoting all his energies to whichever line of business he considers most suited to his particular talents.'

'You know my brother is no business shark!' she flared, aggravated by the certainty that he was contemptuous of Percy. 'Because of you, he has lost his title, his fiancée, his home, most of his friends, and all of his social life! You promised him a directorship, implied that it would be sufficiently well paid to enable him to continue with his social activities, but as things now stand he cannot afford the upkeep of his London flat, much less the cost of feeding and stabling his polo ponies!'

In spite of a glowering presentiment of danger she was caught completely off guard by his painful grip upon her shoulders and by the shaking he administered while condemning through gritted teeth.

'And what about yourself, Morva? What about the sacrifice you were forced to make to further your brother's interests? Or are you still too cowed by family, too brainwashed by tradition, to count the cost of having been tied for the rest of your life to a husband you clearly despise . . .?'

And who despises you!

He had not said that the antipathy was mutual, but the silent implication hung in the air between them causing her to wince, to blink back tears that would have given him the satisfaction of knowing how vulnerable she felt, how easily she fell victim to his caustic tongue. With a choke of despair she turned away from the knight of commerce whose wit stabbed deeply as a lance, whose self-assurance seemed impenetrable as a suit of armour.

Because she was prevented by the presence of workmen from seeking the sanctuary of her old room, she started towards the exotic Oriental suite she had begun to hate as night by solitary night the passion-red interior grew more oppressive. While tossing and turning in the lonely silence the garnet glint of feline eyes seemed to intensify; the sabre-toothed grins of painted dragons seemed gradually to widen as they leered down from the canopy above her bed as if waiting to pounce upon the bride no one wanted—even at a bargain price. . . .

'Oh, no you don't,' Troy's hand descended roughly, halting her in mid flight, 'we have a job to do, remember! If grievances must be nursed they'll have to wait until after working hours.'

The ground floor rooms of the castle were to remain untouched, cleaned and polished, but otherwise left as they had been for centuries. But the first- and second-floor bedrooms were in a state of seige while closets were being converted into bathrooms with ceilings lowered and coved to create a sense of comfort between towering walls, the remaining stretches being tiled and fitted with luxurious bathroom suites, carefully chosen to complement the colour schemes existing in adjacent bedrooms. For the following couple of hours Troy kept her busy scribbling his terse instructions into a notebook as they wandered from room to room accompanied by the architect in charge of alterations.

'The cleaners can begin working in the Mary Stuart Suite first thing tomorrow morning,' Troy ordered her to transcribe once they had completed a tour of rooms decorated with tartan wallcoverings, a peat brown carpet, sheepskin rugs, and drapes and covers of heather-blue velvet.

'The Grey Satin Bedroom should be ready for their attention the following day, then the Chintz, the White Satin, the Blue Satin, the Crystal and Tabberet bedrooms ought to be ready for completion in that order.'

Still desperately scribbling, she followed the two men along a passageway as they continued their inspection, catching them up just as the architect was opening a door leading into the Rose Boudoir.

'I'm not at all certain of the colour scheme proposed for this room, Lord Howgill.' He rifled through a sheaf of notes then quoted from instructions. 'Ceiling white; walls and paintwork washed and painted one coat only to blend with background of covers and curtains. But which colour?' he appealed to Morva. 'Could you offer some guidance, Lady Howgill?'

Troy's tight smile, his attitude of mocking deference when he stood aside to allow her to enter seemed to indicate that he had interpreted her startled reaction to her new title as revulsion, and was annoyed by it.

She strove hard to appear as calm and knowledgeable as her position demanded when she stepped inside the large room dominated by a bed with an enormous pink satin dome suspended overhead, ribbed and frilled and extravagantly ruched, its underside clustered with pink satin bows, rosettes, and tasselled ropes draped low as the hem of rose-patterned bed-curtains.

'Such frivolous folly cries out for a calming influence,' she grimaced apologetically, 'a colour that is light without being frothy. A deep shade of cream might look nice,' she glanced at Troy for confirmation then quickly looked away when his expression warned that he was defying her to reach an independent decision. 'Yes, make it deep cream,' she instructed recklessly, 'on walls, pilasters, cornice, the lot!'

Just as she finished speaking a noise filled the room, a sound that was alien yet vaguely familiar. Its gradually increasing volume drew them towards a window overlooking the grounds.

'A helicopter!' Morva gasped, amazed by the frenzied threshing of bushes and trees fringing the large area of lawn beneath the slowly lowering aircraft. 'Who on earth . . .!'

'Only one person that I can think of!' Troy's features were creased by a wide grin of pleasure. Grabbing her by the wrist he began propelling her out of the room and towards the staircase, giving her no chance to resist, no time to gasp questions as she was raced out of the castle and through the grounds, arriving at the edge of the clearing just as the helicopter landed.

'Aunt Cassie!' he yelled, waving an enthusiastic welcome to a white-haired figure stepping sprightly to the ground, then ducking half double in a effort to combat the draught being caused by still-whirling rotor blades.

'Troy, you young devil!' Morva heard him addressed before he left her standing to sprint across the grass to envelope his unexpected visitor in a crushing bear hug.

She hung back, amused by the bubbling effervescence of Troy's aunt, looking at least twenty years younger than he had intimated, in a bright red cotton safari suit, her silver hair expertly cut and styled, and wearing sandals with slender heels that added at least two inches to her diminutive height.

'Troy, my darling boy, I could hardly believe it when I heard the news!'

'How *did* you hear the news, Aunt Cassie?' He grinned down at her excited face.

'I sent a cablegram to your office in Toronto—thinking that was where you'd most likely be—and thought some joker was sending me up when I received a reply stating: Nephew now tenth Earl of Howgill. Present location ancestral home. Ravenscrag Castle. County of Cumbria. U.K.'

She squeezed him delightedly. 'Naturally, I hopped on to the first available flight leaving Paris for London, then chartered a chopper to fetch me the rest of the way. Oh, and just guess who I've brought with me!' She stood on tip-toe to plant a smacking kiss on his cheek, then turned to wave with a triumphant flourish in the direction of the now silent helicopter.

Morva's glance followed then froze, mesmerised by the vision of beauty picking an elegant course towards Troy. Dimly, her mind registered his aunt's jocular scolding.

'Now, are you prepared to admit what a clever old aunt you have! When I bumped into your girl in Paris I insisted that she should come with me!'

'Troy, darling . . .!' Confidently, the girl slid into

his embrace as if she had been there many times before, then tilted her golden head, inviting his kiss.

Willingly, he obliged, then, wearing an expression Morva could only define as bashful, he slid an arm around each of his visitors' waists to turn them around until all three were facing in her direction.

'Just to prove that you're not the only experts at springing surprises,' he teased in an affectionate drawl, 'I'd like to introduce both of you to my wife.

'Aunt Cassie. Miss Lynda Lewis. Meet Lady Morva Belvoir, Countess of Howgill!'

CHAPTER SIX

For no particular reason that she could think of, Morva was prepared to dislike Lynda Lewis intensely. Not because she was envious of her beauty, she assured herself, nor because she was a rich heiress, the only child of one of Troy's multi-millionaire business colleagues, but because she felt certain that she could not possibly find anything in common with a girl who had allowed herself to become so foolishly besotted with Troy Belvoir that she had been unable to dredge up sufficient pride or strength of composure to disguise the shattering blow she had been dealt when informed of his marriage.

Yet strangely, once introductions had been concluded, questions had been rapidly fired and just as rapidly answered, and the initial surge of excitement had gradually begun to wane, Morva had reluctantly sensed how difficult, almost impossible, it would be to dislike the gentle-voiced girl whose wealthy background appeared to have made little or no impression upon her kind, unspoiled nature. Deep affection for Troy was apparent in every word and glance she directed his way, yet her generosity of spirit was underlined when, after Morva had shown her to her room and was about to take her leave, Lynda halted her in her tracks with the impulsive admission.

'I decided upon a tour of Europe in an effort to get Troy out of my system! I've been in love with him for years,' she confessed simply, 'ever since the day Poppa elected to act as guide through the commercial jungle for the benefit of a young man faced with the responsibility of heading a huge corporation after the premature death of his father, who was Poppa's closest friend. Our friendship never developed into anything deeper—on Troy's part, at least,' she qualified wryly. 'When first we met I was just a schoolgirl, and in spite of all the effort I put into making him see me as an attractive, sophisticated lady I'm afraid that to him I'll always be seen as an unwordly child in need of brotherly protection.'

Her lovely eyes had been deep with feeling when she had assured Morva. 'But in spite of my disappointment, I'm delighted that Troy has fallen in love at last. In common with most individuals who have been blessed, some would say cursed, with a great deal of wealth, he needs the assurance that he is loved as a person and not merely as a provider. I feel certain,' she had concluded with a sincerity that had moved Morva to shame, 'that unlike many of my previous rivals for Troy's affection you are a giver rather than a taker. From you, he will gain all the love and happiness that he deserves. . . .'

Morva was sitting on a balcony overlooking the gardens, mulling over the puzzling new aspect of Troy with a legion of females competing for his attention, when Percy ran her to earth.

'I thought I'd find you in your favourite bolt hole!'

He dropped down beside her on a marble bench, looking more cheerful than she had seen him for weeks.

'You look as if you've just come into a fortune,' she smiled, then immediately regretted the oblique reference to his lack of funds.

'How clever of you to guess the direction in which my thoughts have been leading,' he grinned widely, stooping to adjust the immaculate crease in his trousers. 'But then, haven't you already proved that the quickest way to a fortune is to marry one! People in our position cannot afford to have scruples. If a choice piece of prey should cross our path we feel duty bound to go after it.'

She spread suddenly damp palms over a surface of cold stone, hoping she was wrong in assuming that the prey he had centred in his sights was the recently hurt and consequently very vulnerable Lynda Lewis. But proof that her instinct was correct came as soon as he had settled into a comfortable position, heaving a sigh of satisfaction.

'I have no intention of living like a serf at the beck and call of your husband for twenty-four hours of every day! Not when I can take a short cut to Poppa Lewis's boardroom by catching Troy's lovesick young friend on the rebound. She's a rich young pigeon blown right off course,' he chuckled, 'grieving for a lost mate, and just right for plucking.'

'You're despicable!' Morva accused in a flat monotone that disguised a vortex of outraged emotions. 'In certain circumstances an arranged marriage can be sociably acceptable, but what you are proposing is downright dishonest,' she condemned her complacent brother, 'the act of an unscrupulous gigolo!'

'Come off it, Morva!' he ground between lips twisted into a sneer. 'We've both been raised to believe that hunting is good sport, whether the prey be two-legged or four. You've trapped your fox, why try to deny me the privilege of cornering a vixen?'

'Please don't talk that way, Percy.' She turned aside to hide an expression of disgust, sickened by sudden insight into the way traditions she had been brought up to regard as acceptable might be viewed as contemptuous by visitors from the other side of the Atlantic. 'Why not try putting all your efforts into the career Troy has mapped out for you—you might get to like it, might even become successful enough to allow you to propose marriage to the girl you love.'

'Love!' he scoffed with a smile of derision. 'Love can bestow a very pleasant sense of well-being, I agree, nevertheless, it would be the last reason I would put forward as an argument in favour of matrimony!'

He began sauntering away then hesitated, turning to eye her with a look of uncertainty she found puzzling.

'Oh, by the way, I've been meaning to ask you. . . .' His glance fell away to direct rapt attention upon the toecaps of his elegant shoes. 'How are things between yourself and Belvoir?' He reddened, then soldiered on in the manner of one who had set himself a task and was determined to finish it. 'I'm not such a swine that I can clear my mind of worry about whether Belvoir is gentleman enough to take youth and innocence into consideration when he imposes the physical demands of marriage.'

Morva jumped to her feet, her cheeks flaring as red as her newly discovered temper. She felt stripped of all dignity, betrayed by family and by one member in particular whose conscience had been belatedly aroused by the slamming of her bedroom door.

'Forgive me if I sound cynical, Percy,' she snubbed the childhood idol whose glitter she had mistaken for gold, 'but for you to question Troy's ability to act as a gentleman seems to me as incongruous as a wolf questioning the motives of a tiger!'

She left him looking stunned by a broadside delivered from the very last quarter he had expected, and hurried up to the suite she shared with a husband who, during the short duration of their marriage, had somehow managed to avoid intruding upon her privacy. Frequently, she had spotted signs of his earlier occupation of the bathroom they were forced to share—a razor left upon a shelf; the lingering, astringent scent of the soap he favoured; a damp patch spreading on the mat where he had stood before, with typical male thoughtlessness, dumping the towels he had used in a wet untidy heap upon the floor.

But immediately she entered the sitting room she became aware of sounds of movement behind the dressing-room door. She hurried towards the main bedroom and sidled inside, then stood with her back against the door wondering why her heart should be thumping, why nerves had been stampeded into a state of panic by the close proximity of a man who saw her as no more than a business partner whose services had been secured for the bargain price of a wedding ring.

Unaccountably saddened by the thought, she began slowly undressing, conscious of her duty to be ready to receive guests when they appeared for dinner. She had just slid into her dressing gown and was standing poised, listening to ensure that the connecting bathroom was vacant, when a tap upon the bedroom door sent a startled jolt through her tense frame.

'Come in. . . .' she quavered, knowing that it had to be Troy seeking admittance.

He entered with the hesitancy of a freedom-loving mustang wary of unfamiliar territory, scanning his surroundings in the manner of a stallion anxious to establish all possible escape routes. A strange feeling came over her as she watched him draw nearer. An electric tremor shot along her spine, her pulse began racing as she wondered, madly and wickedly whether she dare act upon a theory that had been advanced in the magazine article she had just finished reading, an article devoted to the findings of scientists who had researched the phenomenon of flirting, studied the meaning behind the wink; the long, tender look; the vital need for physical contact, and the indefinable enchantment that drew together men and women who found one another mutually and sexually attractive.

When it comes to flirting, it is the female who makes the first advances. . . . Men are not leaders, but lemmings in the mating game, a game so ritualised its moves can even be tabulated. Firstly, the female moves her body to attract the male's attention. Secondly, she closes in. This move is repeated several times until she is certain the male is attracted. . . . The first kiss is a prelude to a dramatic synchronised burst of pre-mating love play. . . .

Her knees were shaking, her palms damp, as she forced herself to turn her back, striving to look cool as she sauntered across to the dressing table.

'What can I do for you?' she almost choked the polite enquiry, averting her eyes from a mirror reflecting white-faced panic—lips childishly trembling, wide eyes running scared.

His tone when he explained his intrusion was quiet, unadorned, and sober as his suit.

'I have to beg a favour, Morva.'

'Oh, yes . . .?' she encouraged, fastening a tight grip on the handle of her hairbrush. She saw his image looming behind her own in the mirror and quickly sheered her glance away from a cobalt blue gaze gleaming bright with anxiety.

'Would you mind very much if I were to act out a public show of affection?' Her body seemed to melt beneath the warmth of his breath stroking across the nape of her neck as he bent to seek encouragement from her expression. 'Just an odd kiss or two and an occasional endearment,' he pleaded roughly, 'to soothe Aunt Cassie's suspicious nature. She's all the family I have. Her peace of mind means a great deal to me. Am I asking too much of you, Morva?'

Why beg favours that have already been stolen? she wanted to scream, but instead called upon reserves of dignity and pride to help her pretend that his kisses had not seared, that her treacherous body had not been ignited by his flame, melted by the heat of passion he seemed to be able to manipulate at will, controlled as if by a thermostat set to achieve maximum heat with a minimum amount of effort.

'Of course not,' she lied bravely. 'In fact, one might argue that keeping guests happy is part of our arrangement. Your aunt must already be wondering,' she murmured wistfully, 'why, when the world is filled with birds of brilliant plumage, you should have elected to mate with a plain English sparrow.'

She sensed his outrage and looked up just in time to catch a glimpse of cloud-darkened eyes split by a lightning flash of anger. Then with a tormented growl he clamped his hands upon her shoulders, pulling her into the loose circle of his arms.

'If you are plain,' he spelled out steadily, razing brilliant eyes over a tumble of richly tinted hair, 'then autumn leaves are plain!' His gaze travelled slowly downward, encompassing startled brown eyes, pale unblemished skin, and soft lips trembling around a gasp of sheer surprise, before continuing softly. 'Also creamy camellia petals; berries, sweet ripe and red, and the pride, grace, and intangible *esprit* of the noble thoroughbred which is often copied but seldom successfully, by less genteel mortals. Appreciate your own valuable virtues, Morva, instead of envying the bluebird a colour that is purely illusionary.'

His stormy look faded as he responded gently to her look of puzzlement. 'According to Indian legend, there was a time, before birds were created, when the Great Spirit became depressed each autumn as the trees began shedding their foliage. Then after many colour-starved winters he was inspired by the notion of turning leaves into birds—red leaves into robins, pochards and ruffs; yellow leaves into chiffchaff, titmouse and wagtails, and all remaining leaves into a multitude of birds with mainly black and brown plumage. But as there were no blue leaves the bluebird was left colourless. Squeaking with rage, it flew up to heaven where the Great Spirit lived in order to register a protest. But when he arrived his plumage had turned a deep celestial blue. The fact that the colour was merely a reflection did not matter,' he smiled gravely, 'because the effect upon the bluebird was the same as it would have been had its feathers absorbed blue pigment. He was happy because he felt fulfilled.'

His hands dropped to his sides as he stepped away, putting a width of carpet between them. 'And that is exactly how it will be with you, Morva. Once you have nerved yourself to fly, to reach for your own particular piece of heaven, the sparrow you scorn will be transformed into a bluebird of happiness.'

She stood motionless with hands tightly clasped, struggling to decipher the message contained in his clipped words, but too conscious of electricity crackling in the air between them and of a revival of the inner tumult that had been sparked into life by the first sexual kisses she had ever experienced in her cloistered, female-orientated existence. She had no way of recognising strange emotions as the first stirrings of sexual arousal in a nubile body, slender yet curvaceous, unblemished, untouched, yet ripe for love. Her mind, conditioned from childhood to put pride and modesty first, was dulled by impulses demanding gratification—a divine repetition of her first rapturous physical encounter. . . .

Acting purely upon instinct inherited by all females from their earth mother, Eve, she glided slowly towards him then arched her body against his, lifting soft, inviting lips to be kissed. She felt a quiver run through his tense frame, heard the rasp of a sharply indrawn breath, then melted beneath the warmth of hands exploring the cool velvet slopes of her shoulders.

Then, shockingly, the lapels of her thin silk dressing gown were jerked tightly together, clasped against her throat by a bunched fist. Heavy lashes opened over desire-drugged eyes. She stared, confounded by the message of rejection being transmitted by his hard, angry mouth, by a jawline clenched as if to withstand intolerable strain, and by the choking grip of fingers tightening the silken noose around her neck until the pressure became almost murderous.

'Get dressed, Morva . . .!' The command rasped from stern lips as he pushed her away so violently she stumbled against the dressing table, sending a small crystal perfume flagon crashing to the floor.

Ever afterwards the scent of rosemary, the emblem of remembrance and fidelity in love, was to signify to her the shame of rejection, the shattering of naive ideals that had led her to follow the instinct of a fawning puppy hungry for affection.

Yet an ingrained sense of dignity helped her to pull herself erect, to draw the gaping edges of her dressing gown around her cold, shivering body as she suffered his gritted condemnation, white faced, but with head unbowed.

'Before a fledgling can fly it must first learn to stand and walk and run and climb. The down of innocence cannot be cast off in one day, Morva,' he reminded dully, 'maturity is a slow, lengthy process, a day-by-day growth of flesh, mind, and spirit that makes waiting seem tedious until the time of the maiden flight, the day of lift-off when patience is rewarded by a glorious flight on soaring wings.'

It called for a great deal of courage on her part to wash and change into her best brown dress before joining Troy downstairs to greet their guests as if the shattering scene had not taken place, to have to pretend a composure she did not feel—outwardly smiling, inwardly bleeding, scarred by the shame of having made plain her willingness to discard old loyalties as he had once demanded; humiliated by his rejection of her timid, exploratory advances.

Her pain did not lessen when Lynda's dazzling appearance seemed to provide ample clues to Troy's indifference. She was last to appear on the threshold of the ante room where he was dispensing pre-dinner drinks to the rest of their guests, and stood poised, unselfconsciously anticipating the admiring gasps that followed immediately all eyes became focused upon creamy shoulders left bare by the strapless black velvet bodice of a dress with a taffeta skirt falling into gathers that added a sophisticated rustle to her poised, slightly swaying walk.

Morva's heart contracted with an envy she found impossible to control when, with visible relief, Troy abandoned his role of referee between his aunt and the Dowager Lady Howgill who had generated antagonism upon their first moment of meeting. He hurried across the room with arms outstretched to clasp a hand around each of her wrists, gazing deeply into her eyes as he drew her slowly forward.

'You look stunning!' His voice held a note of startled admiration. 'At this monent, I find it hard to believe that you were once the child who used to search my pockets for candy whenever I visited your home.'

'Girls grow up quicker than most men will acknowledge,' Lynda responded wistfully. 'Chivalrous types, such as yourself, Troy, are apt to be over-cautious, over-protective in their attitude towards members of what you fondly refer to as the "weaker sex".'

Morva watched in silence, unhappily aware of the chemistry that appeared to have been generated by a spark of recognition that had come—so far as Lynda was concerned—just a few short weeks too late.

Then with an unladylike snort of derision, Aunt Cassie intruded into their absorption.

'It is not chivalry, but chauvinism that motivates men's possessive attitude towards their womenfolk!' she asserted with a belligerence that caused Lady

Howgill a pained wince. 'Whether Oriental potentates or mustang stallions, males like to bolster their egos by surrounding themselves with harems of docile females who allow themselves to be herded, bullied and dominated by men anxious to advertise their boss-man status. Even you, Troy, much as I admire your qualities of strength and leadership, have annoyed me in the past by betraying an unfortunate tendency to treat most members of my sex like helpless dolls with little between their ears but plastic padding!

'I do hope, Morva,' she turned to insist, 'that if ever you should find your husband's chauvinist mentality becoming particularly unbearable, you will be quick to remind him, as I often have, that over a century ago pioneering wives earned themselves the right to be treated as equal partners by tramping alongside covered wagons, through prairies and plains and mountain passes, enduring raids by Indians; hunger, thirst, and deadly fatigue without a murmur of complaint about uncombed hair, ragged clothes, or the utter dearth of civilised amenities! Take my advice, dear, and stake your claim now on the top of his list of priorities, otherwise you could find yourself relegated to the status of squaw who has been conditioned to accept that heaven to an Indian brave consists of horses, buffalo and woman—in that order!'

Morva was saved the embarrassment of having to try to disguise the fact that her status in Troy's eyes was already lower than a squaw, who at least enjoyed the privilege of physical communion with her husband, when Troy rebuked his aunt a trifle dryly.

'Don't you ever tire of mounting your favourite soapbox, Aunt Cassie? You're entitled to state your opinions, of course, but when you do I wish you would try to remember that not every female possesses the talents to make her own way in the world.' Morva stiffened, conscious of the glance he had flicked in her direction. 'Some women need to be supported, just like trees whose survival is dependent upon the bondage of the soil.'

Carefully, Morva set down her untouched glass of wine, hoping to forestall his aunt's counter-attack by requesting that they should all go into dinner. But Percy, who had been keeping score of the number of smiles exchanged between Troy and his beautiful young guest made a determined play for Lynda's attention.

'Personally,' he drawled, looking perfectly at home and extremely handsome as he strolled across a room whose intimidating splendour formed part of his natural setting. 'I consider any young lady who insists upon being regarded as man's equal is missing out.' Gallantly he bowed when he reached Lynda's side and brought a blush to her cheeks by flattering shamelessly. 'Why should any member of your fair sex have to step down from her pedestal in order to redress the balance of prestige between the sexes?'

Either because she found his charm irresistible, or because her badly bruised feelings were soothed by the obvious admiration of a suave, polished member of the aristocracy, Lynda fell immediate victim to Percy's barrage of charm that kept her enthralled all during dinner.

Morva picked at her food, fretting over her brother's motives, very conscious of Troy's clamped-down anger as he played the role of polite host, lightly catching and tossing the conversational ball which, for most of the time, seemed to soar over the heads of the engrossed couple. Not even his aunt's brash handling of her acutely displeased grandmother—whom she insisted upon addressing as Lucy—seemed to amuse him, Morva thought miserably, wishing the meal were over so that she might escape to her room.

'No doubt, Troy, you intend taking Morva home to Canada when you embark upon a belated honeymoon?' His aunt's tone was sharp, as if she too had become aware of and was questioning the reason behind the oppressive atmosphere.

Immediately, he made an effort to allay her curiosity by putting into action the plan that had been formulated for just such an occasion.

'Naturally,' he nodded, directing Morva a smile that rendered her breathless, as if her heart had been suddenly squeezed, 'but as I've already explained, Aunt Cassie,' he continued smoothly, 'we can't spare the time for a honeymoon just yet. There is so much work still to be done here, so many problems requiring personal attention.'

'Fiddlesticks!' The keen-eyed old lady looked stubborn. 'Nothing is more important than a honeymoon, don't you agree, Lucy?' she appealed, ignoring her contemporary's expression of high hauteur. 'Once the hotel project gets off the ground there's no reason why you, I, and your grandson Percy should not all pitch in to give the newly-weds a break!'

Seemingly oblivious to the glare of outrage being directed by the Dowager Countess, she trained a determined look upon Morva.

'You'll love Canada, honey, especially our ranch at the foot of the Rockies which is Troy's permanent base, the place where he chooses to relax whenever he finds an opportunity to jump off the commercial bandwagon. But I've no doubt he'll be eager to show you the places he loves best, to take you right into the heart of the Rockies where he used to camp as a boy and where, during his wild, roistering adolescence, he worked all the wildness out of his system—learning how to fell trees from tough lumberjacks; how to stalk game from cunning trappers; how to bait a tempting line from wily fishermen and most important of all, how to "play possum" from Indians whose infinite patience and wisdom enables them to wait, sometimes for a small eternity, until the tide of fortune turns in their favour.'

She chuckled softly, not one whit disturbed by her nephew's growing discomfiture.

'I'm always amused whenever I think of the day my sister—Lord rest her gentle soul—rounded on Troy's father for the first time in twenty years of marriage, accusing him of turning their only son into a hobo by granting him three years of unrestricted freedom. But my brother-in-law, as well as being an astute businessman, was also a student of human nature, and his assertion that lessons learned in the wild could apply equally as well to the jungle-world of business has been amply justified.'

'So your mother is dead?' Morva consoled Troy, her soft heart aching with pity for the woman who had not lived to enjoy the pride she would have felt for her only son.

'Yes, little sparrow,' he brought a smile of pleasure to his aunt's face by reaching for Morva's hand to feather a kiss over trembling fingertips, 'that is yet another thing we have in common.'

Her grandmother jerked to attention. Unused to being a listener instead of a dictator, she snapped.

'Morva's mother is not dead, she's simply not welcome in this house!'

Morva felt Troy's clasp tighten, but his drawl was bland to the point of boredom when he apologised.

'Forgive me, I must have misunderstood. Morva and I have spent so little time in private, it's hardly surprising that gaps should occur in our knowledge of each other's personal history. If you would excuse us,' he rose from the table, retaining his clasp upon her wrist so that she was forced to rise with him, 'I'll take my wife for a stroll around the grounds where we can perhaps remedy a few omissions.'

Only she recognised the thread of threat running through his words, a thread that seemed stretched taut as elastic by the time he had guided her through French windows opening out into the garden, then along a stretch of pathway leading away from the house towards a sunken, secluded rose garden.

He wasted no time on preliminaries, but charged her with deceit the moment they were hidden from sight, surrounded by shrubs laden with heady, heavily scented roses.

'You implied that you were an orphan!'

'I'm as good as,' she hedged her eyes nervously downcast, envying a sparrow its ability to fly from the sound of unfriendly voices. 'My mother deserted me when I was an infant and I'm pleased she did—she is a wicked, selfish, immoral woman!'

'If you were a mere infant when she left, how can you possibly judge?'

She raised puzzled eyes to meet his demanding stare. 'Why . . . because Granny has told me all about her of course!'

She faltered into silence, faced, the moment the

admission was voiced, by her very first doubts about the mother who, by Granny's own admission, had never been made welcome at Ravenscrag.

'Oh, Morva!' he sighed, pinning her shoulders between his hands to administer a gentle shake so far removed from his earlier rough handling she felt pushed to the edge of tears. 'What a confused, bewildered, *lost*, young creature you are! A mixture of gullible child and composed aristocrat, timid mouse and fearless equestrian ... terrified bride, and brazen would-be seducer.' He tilted her chin, forcing her to withstand his softly growled challenge.

'Who am I married to Morva? How can I decide which one of many complex characters is my wife?'

She stared back dumbly, unable to find words to explain the tumult of mixed emotions that was hiding the answer even from herself.

He released her, looking suddenly weary.

'Forget that question. And please don't worry, the situation will sort itself out. Remember only that patience is a bitter plant, but its fruit is sweet and infinitely delicious. . . .'

CHAPTER SEVEN

THE builders had finished. All traces of their occupation had been removed from luxurious bathrooms, from a modernised kitchen fitted with every conceivable appliance designed to increase efficiency and ease of management, and from rooms and corridors made draught proof and warm by a super-efficient heating and ventilating system. Yet on the surface nothing seemed changed, Morva decided as she wandered through ground-floor rooms checking work carried out by newly employed cleaning ladies who had rushed to respond to advertisements posted throughout neighbouring villages. Extra outside staff had also been enrolled, gardeners, gamekeepers, and farmworkers whose job it would be to ensure that a plentiful supply of home-cured bacon, fresh eggs, butter, cream and vegetables could be included in daily menus.

Troy seemed as pleased as a child with a new toy, she smiled, stooping to examine ancient brocade curtains whose bald patches had been expertly darned with gold and silver thread. No expense had been spared, no luxury omitted from the castle whose linen-room shelves were freshly stocked with sheets, pillowcases, napkins and towels; whose cellars were lined with bottles of choice vintage wines from many different countries to appease many different palates; whose servants' quarters were shortly due to be filled to capacity with resident chambermaids, housemaids and footmen—with every grade of helper, in fact, that had been employed in the days when Ravenscrag had been noted among the nobility as a place in which to enjoy generous hospitality, glittering balls, and delicious dinners to round off days spent hunting, shooting and fishing, or simply relaxing in peaceful, comfortable surroundings.

'Morva, honey!' Aunt Cassie's bustling figure intruded into her reverie. 'You did say that it would be all right for Lynda to move into the Rose Boudoir? The girl's taken such a shine to that room! If you've no objection, I'd like to move her things in there before she gets back from London. When *is* she coming back, by the way? I must say, I was very surprised when Troy raised no objection to your brother's plan to show Lynda the sights of the capital during this breathing space before the Grand Opening. I'm really looking forward to it, aren't you?' She clasped both hands together in an excess of excited anticipation. 'It's such a thrill feeling useful again. I'm not cut out for a life of leisure. My doctor declares he's never seen so much energy contained in one small body. He keeps telling me to slow down, to act my age, but I like to act the way I feel which, at this moment, is rejuvenated by Troy's surrender to my plea to be allowed to stay and help get this show on the road. I'm so grateful to him—and to you, too, honey,' she hastened to add. 'I keep forgetting that Ravenscrag has been home to your family for decades. Are you very upset at the thought of it being turned into a very grand, up-market hotel?'

Morva waited for a break in the old lady's barrage of questions. She had grown used to coping with spates of rapidly fired comments, to her habit of starting on one subject then going off at a tangent, covering a whole spectrum of topics while barely pausing to draw breath.

She began at the beginning. 'No, of course I don't mind your moving Lynda's belongings in the Rose Boudoir, how could I when she's so set upon becoming the first guest to be entered into our official Register? And yes, I do know that she and Percy will be returning in good time for my brother to practise his duties as controller of the wine cellar well before the first quota of guests arrive. Yesterday, during a very brief telephone conversation, I gained the impression that they were both having a great deal of fun,' she confided a trifle wistfully. 'Since his late teens, Percy has lived most of the time in his London flat, paying only short flying visits to Ravenscrag. Consequently, he has become very much a part of the social scene, so I've no doubt that Lynda will be wining and dining at parties given by whichever socialites have not yet joined the migratory flock that heads each July for St Tropez and Monte Carlo. It would have been most unkind of Troy to have attempted to prevent her from enjoying such an experience. And yet,' a thoughtful frown creased her brow, 'Lynda is surprisingly strong-willed, I doubt whether she would allow Troy to dictate her movements.'

'Troy has no wish to dictate anyone's movements!' Her heart leapt, as it always did whenever she caught sight of his powerful frame clad in the rodeo rider's uniform of checked shirt and well-worn denims. 'He's a strong defender of liberty,' he continued rebuking as he strolled into the room, 'who believes in allowing people to make their own mistakes then quickly learn to make them good. If Lynda prefers to spend her time in the company of a sybarite who chooses to live an unreal life among unreal people rather than join the world of harsh reality populated by less-privileged mortals, she is entitled to do so.'

'You're not being fair!' A sense of injustice forced Morva to defend her absent brother. 'I'm certain Percy has surprised himself, as well as the rest of us, by displaying an enthusiasm for the job he has been allocated. He's been studying the Bartenders' Guide in order to add to his already considerable knowledge of cocktails; has made notes of what to serve if ever he should be asked for a hangover cure, or a pick-me-up, and has even spent time creating decorative effects with lemon, orange, cherries, mint and borage sprigs. Because we'll all be forced to work non-stop once the first lot of guests arrive, he's entitled to a little fun and relaxation during what might be termed the lull before the storm.'

'That's telling him, gal!' Aunt Cassie almost whooped her approval. Then she scowled at Troy. 'That last statement of Morva's makes a lot of sense to me, and if you weren't such a beavering businessman you'd have no need to be reminded that all members of staff work better after a relaxing break—including your wife,' she stressed meaning-fully, 'who, from what little I've seen of her this past couple of weeks appears to have been putting as much effort as yourself into learning the hotel business.'

Her inference was so plain Morva blushed, hoping he would not think she had been angling for time off to spend a few hours away from work that had captured her interest to such an extent that even time spent exercising Clio had begun shrinking shorter and shorter.

'Well now, Aunt Cassie, you must have been reading my mind!' he grinned, strolling casually forward until he was close enough to pluck a clipboard and pencil from Morva's nerveless fingers.

'Whatever else you have planned to do can wait,' he instructed in the manner of a masterful husband, 'I'll allow you fifteen minutes to pretty yourself up for a visit to a house across the border belonging to a business colleague of mine. He and his wife are expecting us for lunch. So if you can, wear something light,' he mocked sardonically, 'something less like a compulsory school uniform.'

It was a fairly lengthy journey from Ravenscrag to the equally isolated spot just over the Scottish border to which, Troy had told her, his colleague retreated as often as he was able from the noise and turmoil of London's Stock Exchange. But the moment she slid into the plump, leather-bound passenger seat she knew she was going to enjoy every minute of the drive in what must surely have been one of the world's most luxurious motors—a no-expense-spared dream of refinement and superb craftsmanship that had levers that responded at a touch to adapt front seats to individual standards of comfort. Noiseless air conditioning maintained ideal temperatures in both the upper and lower levels of the car, but the ultimate extravagance, so far as she was concerned, was the fitted cabinet containing everything necessary for mixing perfect cocktails.

For the better part of an hour Troy drove in silence, allowing her to revel in the pleasure of cruising silently and smoothly along deserted moorland roads, through quiet country lanes lined with trees meeting overhead to form cool green tunnels, dappled with sunshine and filled with the scent of wild flowers massed along verges. Then when the sun had reached its noonday peak, he delighted her by pressing a button to activate motors which stealthily slid back the roof until they were driving with only clear blue sky overhead, fully exposed to the sounds and smells of the countryside and to a breeze that felt like a gentle hand brushing past glowing cheeks, ruffling through a long mane of hair left loose to tumble past her shoulders, a shiny, velvet brown stream with strands tinted red, gold and amber by probing fingers of sunshine.

At the sound of an ecstatic sigh Troy cast her a smiling sideways glance that encompassed every detail of her pleasantly relaxed body, looking cool and curvaceous in a pink-and-white candystripe dress made of slightly outmoded seersucker, with tiny cap sleeves and a plunging, V-shaped neckline made prim where it should have tantalised by a row of tiny buttons fastened into scalloped edging reaching down to a narrow white belt clasped around an incredibly slender waist.

'It takes so little to please you, Morva,' he teased, 'I hardly dare dwell upon your likely reaction to a gift of diamonds or exotic furs!'

'Which would be much the same as old Tom's, Clio's regular blacksmith, I imagine,' she giggled, feeling wickedly spoiled but utterly contented.

'Some misguided person was moved to offer an old smithy a gift of diamonds or furs?' he encouraged in a tone of mock astonishment.

'Of course not!' Her giggle escalated into a trill of spontaneous laughter that sparked an appreciative glint into his watchful eyes. 'Tom was merely commenting with customary sourness upon the imminent invasion of his territory by the newly rich who, in his opinion, are disciples of the devil sent to fill Ravenscrag with "muckle din and gigglin" hizzys—sparsely clad women, and men who've neither thought nor care for the Sabbath when they lust after sportive leisure.'

Her smile faded when suddenly she realised the dangerous direction into which her tongue had strayed.

'I'm sorry,' she winged a fleeting glance over his inscrutable features, 'it was very tactless of me to repeat the remarks of a bigoted old countryman who fears his long-established peace is about to be destroyed by hordes of jaded tourists determined to squeeze some sort of thrill from their wealth.'

'You speak as if you despise riches, as if you consider wealthy people an unfortunate minority deserving of compassion,' he mused dryly, almost as if he were thinking aloud. 'If wealth is a wasting disease without any known cure,' he continued deliberately, 'why does the creed that you live by dictate that the main object of marriage should be financial gain?'

She coloured, shrinking as small as she was able into the leather-bound cocoon.

'But not necessarily personal gain,' she reminded painfully, 'and only when family circumstances warrant such a drastic course of action.'

For thoughtful seconds he remained silent then, in the same casual way in which he steered the purring car around an awkward corner, he challenged.

'Tell me truthfully, Morva. Given another time, another existence, could you ever envisage being happily married to a Canadian backwoodsman with nothing to offer except the wages of hard graft and a powerfully strong yearning for children?'

'No, never,' she blushed, unhappily convinced that even in another existence her luck would deny her any such blessings, then lapsed into tongue-tied confusion, puzzled by the frown that had descended upon his features, making his out-thrust jaw seem cast from a mould of iron.

As if eager to adapt to his morose mood, the sun disappeared behind a patch of grey cloud so that a frown seemed suddenly to have been cast over the countryside. When a raindrop, heavy as a solitary tear, splashed on to the back of hands held trembling in her lap he glanced sideways, then with a muttered imprecation that caused her to curl tighter into her seat, he pressed a button to activate the roof back to its previous position, shutting out scents, sounds and all sensations of movement.

Feeling as if a door had been slammed, enclosing her within a tomb of brooding silence, she turned her head aside to concentrate her attention upon a blurred impression of fields and hedges that began racing faster and faster as he increased pressure on the accelerator. She shivered, miserably aware that she had somehow managed to offend him, but completely at a loss to understand a mood that seemed to deepen with the deterioration of the outside atmopshere—a gradual massing and lowering of clouds that grew darker and more oppressive as they drove nearer to the border.

Lightning, warning that a storm was imminent, flashed from a brassy sky and flickered over the roofs of solitary farmhouses and dark green forests as they drove through the Scottish lowlands. Thunder echoed around mist-shrouded hills and rolled across acres of grassland dotted with sheep huddled in groups, seeking the comfort of fellow creatures as they bleated timid mistrust of threatening elements.

Envying them their warm animal contact, Morva remained still and quiet, watching large coindrops of rain splashing on to the bonnet of the car, then jerked with alarm when Troy broke his silence with the terse observation.

'We've almost arrived at our destination. The house is hidden from the road by a belt of trees, but any minute now we should see a sign indicating our approach to a concealed drive. Keep a sharp look-out just in case it should be missed—I don't relish the thought of being lost in stormy, unfamiliar country-side.'

Flicking the windscreen wipers into action he slowed down to a crawl, then a few minutes later nodded approval of her vigilance when she spotted a warning notice rendered almost invisible by rambling briars and creeping stems of honeysuckle.

'Slow down, there's an opening about fifty yards to the left!'

At first sight, the house that loomed at the end of a long, carefully tended drive appealed to Morva as the most welcoming sight she had ever seen. Even with a backcloth of lowering clouds and rain falling like a veil across bellied chimneypots and heavy ornamental gutters, its appeal remained, heightened by windows with curtains drawn back to create a bright golden flare path for the guidance of visitors. The old grey stone manse had an aura of family unity, a beckoning, arms-open-wide encouragement to enter that seemed amply borne out by the woman who flung the door open wide, whose breathless, almost sobbed greeting, seemed to indicate that their appearance had heralded the climax to hours of nail-biting anticipation.

'Troy, at last! How lovely to see you!'

'And you, Bunty!' He stooped to kiss the cheek of their hostess who was staring straight past him, her gaze fixed unwaveringly upon Morva's shy, hesitant approach. Troy beckoned her forward. 'Bunty, I'd like you to meet——'

'Morva . . .!' She heard her name escape softly as a sigh from their hostess's lips, and grew even more puzzled when she waved Troy to silence and concluded simply. 'I would have known her any-where!'

Then as if making a tremendous effort to regain her composure, she added hastily. 'From your description, of course. Come inside out of the rain, my dear.' She held out a beringed, elegant, manicured hand towards her. 'My husband, Alan, is dying to meet you—and please call me Bunty, everyone does.'

Morva did not need to try to relax, but lost her shyness completely in the company of the mature, smartly dressed woman and her equally charming though rather more elderly husband who appeared seconds later to shake Troy by the hand and to kiss Morva's cheek immediately introductions had been effected.

'Welcome, my dear,' he smiled kindly, 'I hope that this is just the first of many frequent visits to our home.'

The instant affinity Morva felt at first meeting grew stronger during an inteval spent pleasantly chatting over a delicious lunch, and intensified to surprising proportions when Troy and Alan absented themselves in order to discuss the business matter that had made their meeting necessary.

She and Bunty made their way to a cosy sitting room and relaxed into armchairs set either side of an old-fashioned log fire.

'Ah, that's better!' Bunty kicked off her shoes and stretched luxuriously. 'Now, my dear, we can really get down to the business of making friends.' She hesitated, then seemingly encouraged by Morva's expression of contentment, proceeded cautiously. 'I hope you won't think me presumptuous if I ask you a rather personal question?'

Her look was so anxious, so genuinely kind, that Morva did not hesitate.

'I'm certain your sensitive nature would not allow you to ask personal questions without a very sound reason. What do you wish to know?'

Eagerly, Bunty leant forward. 'Whether you are happy,' she asked simply. 'Whether your marriage to Troy has surrounded you with love and security—has compensated a motherless, abandoned child for a lack of sympathy, understanding and deep affection?'

Morva jerked rigid, her brown eyes stunned by the shocking realisation that her whole life, past, present and most probably future, had been analysed by Troy and the woman who, up until a couple of hours ago, had been a complete stranger. Intolerable hurt welled up inside of her, an unbearable feeling that she had been betrayed by a husband who had proved himself heartlessly indifferent to any embarrassment caused by casual gossip.

Feeling immeasurably cheapened, she jumped to her feet to choke the accusation. 'Troy had no right . . . no right at all to betray such confidences, to discuss my background with a total stranger!'

'Oh, my dear!' In spite of her distress, Morva was struck by Bunty's agonised expression when she rushed to console her. 'Please forgive my clumsy approach! For weeks now, ever since Troy sought me out, I've been rehearsing the opening to our conversation, wondering how best to gain your confidence and eventually—if I should be so blessed— your love. But I cannot allow you to think badly of Troy,' she gasped, brushing away tears that had doused every glint of happiness from frightened grey eyes. 'I simply could not live with the thought of having caused you further pain, of destroying your life for the second time around. Believe me,' she gulped, 'Troy has never once mentioned your childhood to me!' She grasped Morva by the shoulders and shook her urgently. 'He didn't need to, my darling—*I'm your mother!*'

Instinctively, Morva recoiled from the presence of the woman who since early childhood had been depicted in her mind as the evil stepmother or the wicked witch in every lurid fairy tale. Hail battering on the windowpanes filled the darkened room with an ominous drumming, fast as her heartbeats, as she stood frozen with horror, staring at the mother who had been reduced to a weeping trembling wreck by an expression on her daughter's face she had judged to be loathing.

'I'm sorry you dislike me so much, Morva,' she sobbed, turning her tear-drenched face aside. 'Obviously our meeting is a dreadful mistake. But Troy seemed so certain of its success. . . .' Her voice trailed into silence as she stumbled back to her chair and sat with head bowed, fighting to control an ague of trembling.

'What has Troy to do with us?' Morva demanded stonily. 'I understood that a business arrangement between himself and your husband had made this visit necessary.'

When Bunty shook her head and lifted her shoulders in a dejected shrug Morva jerked, recognising one of her brother's mannerisms, realising why she had felt such instant affinity with a woman she had met as a stranger but who was actually her own flesh and blood.

'Our husbands did not meet until very recently. Troy has visited us only once before, on the day he was led here after weeks of enquiry about the whereabouts of your mother.

'It was he who managed to convince me,' she swallowed hard, 'that a reconciliation was essential, that you needed my love even more than I needed yours. That was the only argument,' she stated simply, 'that managed to change my mind about staying out of your life even though, on the day I was persuaded that for your own good I must never see you again, my heart was torn in two and a half of it left in your keeping.'

'You were *persuaded*?' Morva queried, shaken in spite of misgivings, by her mother's sincerity. 'By whom . . .?'

'My dear,' she sighed, 'do you really need to ask? By your grandmother, who else . . .?'

Looking utterly worn out, Bunty leant back until her brown hair, tinted a shade or two redder than Morva's, was spread against a chair cushion, then she closed her eyes and confessed in a dull, expressionless monotone.

'I've been a very bad mother to my only daughter.

Percy, I'm certain, will remember me with affection, because for the first twenty years of my marriage to your father I tried my utmost to be a good wife and mother, to make the best of a marriage whose hasty beginning was followed by years of bitter repentance. But by the time you made an appearance, my darling—the daughter I had always yearned for, whose love and companionship were to make twenty years of hell seem worthwhile,' she murmured, held rapt by memories so absorbing she did not register the sound of Morva's weak-kneed collapse into a chair, 'the war your grandmother had been waging to regain complete domination over your father had been won.'

Restlessly, she stirred. 'I can't bear to go into details,' she decided, firming a mouth that quivered with pain, 'but a brief synopsis of your father's existence would probably read: A schoolboy repressed by a dominating mother. A teenager made prematurely staid by responsibilities inherited upon the death of his father. A young man bemused by his first taste of freedom, let loose among the devil-take-tomorrow youth of wartime Britain with disastrous and far reaching results. A middle-aged man,' she concluded bitterly, 'who chose to live the life of a recluse rather than face a battery of maternal reproaches and a wife and son whose presence was a permanent thorn pricking his conscience!'

A wave of remorse lifted Morva to her feet and carried her towards the crumpled, white-faced woman who appeared to have aged twenty years in as many minutes. Noiselessly she slid down on to her knees to stare into the face of a mother who was oblivious to her close proximity. Suspecting that the picture her grandmother had painted might have been deliberately distorted, she eyed her kindly, freed of all the bitterness she had felt, all the doubts she had nurtured—except one.

'Mother!' she shook her gently. 'How could any mother be persuaded to desert her infant daughter?'

Lids lifted slowly over eyes glowing with wonder, and also a lingering shadow of doubt about whether she had misheard the forgiving form of address. Tentatively, timidly, her hands reached out to cup Morva's face between her palms.

'Because I was judged the guilty party when the divorce suit was heard, your father was granted custody of his daughter, whereas I was allowed access to visit just once a month. Because for the first three years of your life you and I had been inseparable, you became more and more agitated at the end of each visit, consequently, I had to force myself to accept, even before the solicitor's letter and the doctor's report arrived, that only a complete separation would lessen your heartbreak. But although I had to stop visiting, I never stopped loving my baby,' she almost crooned. 'Never has a child been so loved, never has a daughter so occupied her mother's thoughts. Right up until this present year,' she confided with a laugh that lodged halfway in her throat, 'I've bought you a present each Christmas and every birthday. There's a room upstairs reserved exclusively for my daughter's possessions,' she urged shakenly, 'would you like to see it?'

The question hung in the air between them, the words prosaic, yet the meaning behind them of terrific importance to the woman who was waiting to be told whether she was to be accepted as a mother, and to the lonely, rejected girl who had thought herself unloved

and was having great difficulty coming to terms with
the notion of being a loved, adored, only daughter.
Even the storm outdoors seemed momentarily to
abate, ceased rattling hail against the windowpanes as
if anxious to overhear Morva's shyly whispered
acceptance.

'Yes, please, Mother, I should love to see *my* room.'

CHAPTER EIGHT

MORVA fell blissfully in love with the dainty, feminine appeal of the room that was such a marked contrast to the hateful Chinese bridal suite, and to the bedroom she had occupied previous to her marriage that had contained less comfort than cheerless Victorian servants' quarters.

It became obvious the moment she stepped inside that her mother had expiated a burden of grief and frustration by creating a spring-fresh, flowered-chintz shrine to her lost daughter, the passing of each lonely year marked by objects appropriate to her age—from soft, cuddly toys, up to and including roller skates, a tennis racket, and even a beginner's kit of make-up— that were crammed on to windowseats, ranged around walls, and lovingly positioned on top of a peach-frilled, kidney-shaped dressing table.

In an absolute tizzy of excitement her mother pulled open drawers and cupboards, unearthing a positive treasure trove of carefully chosen presents.

'I bought this fan in Madrid for your fifteenth birthday.' She flicked her wrist and posed with a spread of white hand-painted silk held close to her face so that laughing eyes were peeping over a rim of ivory spokes tipped with tiny diamonds.

'This mantilla I spotted in Rome a year later is a perfect match for the fan, don't you think?' She draped a fall of white, exquisitely worked lace over Morva's head and together they bent down to admire the result in the dressing-table mirror. Smiling expressions changed to looks of wonder as they stared at their twin reflections, noting remarkable similarities of bone structure, hairline, and the identical shape and colour of brown eyes made soulful even as they glowed by shadows of past pain captured in their depths.

'I wish I could have seen you on your wedding day, my darling.' Her mother's lips quivered while their glances held. 'I've spent hours mooning over how you must have looked as a bride, how sweet and innocently appealing.'

She jerked upright, abruptly breaking the spell. 'At least there is one gift that can be presented at an appropriate time. Well almost ...!' she qualified, hastening to open the door of a fitted wardrobe that filled the entire length of one wall. 'All these are yours,' she assured her bemused, wide-eyed daughter, swishing a hand across a colourful burst of silk, taffeta, cotton, organza, satin and lace spilling from hangers suspended from a centre rail, 'but hopefully, you will consider this the *pièce de resistance*, a dainty addition to your wedding trousseau.'

'Mother, please stop,' Morva protested weakly, 'I'm completely overwhelmed! The gifts are all beautiful,' she swept an encompassing hand around the bedroom, 'and I can't tell you how much I appreciate your generosity, but there's far too much—I would need to live to be a hundred to wear all those clothes! And in any case,' she concluded gently, 'I need time to appreciate the greatest gift of all. The mother I thought had been lost forever. . . .'

With a sob of gratitude that made words superfluous, her mother consigned a diaphanous confection of cream satin nightwear to the floor and ran to enfold Morva within a loving hug.

'I can hardly believe my luck.' She blinked back tears of happiness. 'Not every mother is blessed with a daughter who is loving and forgiving. And wise too.' Then briskly she pulled herself together. Flinging an arm around Morva's shoulders, she guided her out of the bedroom, hesitating on the threshold to cast a backward glance and to assure a trifle ruefully. 'I've gained a great deal of pleasure and comfort from this room, but I suppose its contents could be construed as bribery, a planned attempt to buy an estranged daughter's affection. That is far from the case, but if you should have any doubts Alan will no doubt tell you—as he has often told me in the past—that I'm apt to swamp those I love with floods of affection. To me, loving is inextricably bound up with giving so I'm afraid, dear child, you've no option but to learn to float with the tide.'

They heard the muffled sound of thunder rumbling overhead as they went in search of their husbands and found them standing in front of the sitting-room window eyeing the theatrical effects of lightning silhouetting surrounding pine forests, and a deluge of rain turning flower beds into ponds and paths into sloping torrents.

'Alan, dear,' Bunty reproved as she and Morva fumbled their way across the darkened room, 'it's so gloomy in here, please turn on the lights.'

Immediately both men turned to offer assistance.

'It's no use,' Alan explained, 'the storm has brought down the power lines and we've been temporarily cut off. Even the 'phone is out of order.'

'Oh, good!' she exclaimed, making no attempt to

hide her delight. 'That means Morva and Troy will have to stay the night.'

Immediately, Morva's eyes sought for Troy's reaction, but shadows had made his features unreadable. His tone, however, was calmly confident, 'I've driven through worse storms than this back home. I'm certain we'll make it back to Ravenscrag.'

'I don't doubt that you have,' Alan cautioned, 'but you must bear in mind that roads in Canada, and especially in the Rockies, have been designed to cope with a variety of weather conditions, where as here in Britain, where the erratic climate can run the gamut of four seasons within the space of one day, roads can be rendered impassable in hours by flooded dips and fords!'

'Then the argument is settled!' Bunty forestalled the protest she sensed might be imminent. 'I just love the idea of Morva's bedroom being brought into use. I'll just slip and tell Cook there'll be two extra for dinner, mercifully, we cook by gas and not electricity.'

'But I've no change of clothing,' Troy's attempt to forestall her held a hint of desperation.

'As if that matters! You are family, dear boy. I don't care what you're wearing, it's your company I want at dinner.'

'If you're worried about pyjamas, I've plenty of spare sets.' Alan's grin conveyed the sympathy of a man who had learned to surrender with good grace to his wife's determined pressure.

'Troy doesn't wear pyjamas,' Morva responded absently, her mind absorbed with the problem of how to fit a man of his size into a chintz, toy, and bric-à-brac filled bedroom without courting some giant-sized disaster.

The appealing naivete of her remark was forçibly rammed home by a conserted chorus of laughter. Even Troy was grinning, amused by the mortification that caused her to blush and stammer.

'What I really meant to say was I've never actually seen him wearing——'

'No need to elaborate, honeybunch,' Troy drawled a warning, strolling to increase her confusion by dropping a tender kiss on to her woebegone mouth. She responded to his cue by offering no resistance when he pulled her into his arms, realising that his fond action was a ploy to enable him to whisper urgently into her ear.

'I guess we'll have to stay. Do you mind . . .?'

Somehow she forced herself to respond with a negative shake of her head before he released her to address their smiling audience.

'You win, Bunty. Your daughter and I accept with pleasure your kind invitation to stay overnight.'

Bunty spent the next couple of hours excitedly hogging the conversation, outlining in detail the happiness inspired by the recent reunion and the many plans she had drawn up for future occasions. Looking totally relaxed, both men sat with legs stretched out towards a roaring log fire, listening patiently, contributing little to the conversation but an occasional grunt or nod, stirring only to set a flaring match to the bowl of a fragrant briar.

Morva, too, sat silent with her feet curled up beneath her and her head resting in the hollow of a winged armchair, trying once again to analyse the exciting, nerve-tingling, pulse racing sensations that had been aroused from their shallow resting place by Troy's perfunctory kiss.

'Troy,' vaguely, Morva's mind registered her mother's note of pleading, 'please describe to me exactly how Morva looked on her wedding day!' Then was startled to attention by his lazy drawl.

'Like a ghostly replica of her grandmother as she looked on *her* wedding day, I should imagine. A prudish Edwardian maiden primed to submit meekly to her husband's physical demands, but kept tightly buttoned, laced, and corseted, as if to ensure that his patience would evaporate long before his passion. Also, the white lace wings she wore swept back from her face reminded me of a sight commonly seen in continental market places where limp young doves are laid in rows, each one plucked, trussed and dressed to titillate the appetite of some insensitive gourmet.'

'I was not corseted!' Morva flashed, incensed by the scornful sketch he had drawn.

'Well, perhaps not,' he conceded with a teasing grin, 'but I assure you, the effect was the same as if you had been.'

A rumble of amusement disturbed Alan's inert frame. 'Nothing much can go wrong with a marriage between two people who share the same sense of humour,' he assured his completely hoodwinked wife.

She nodded happily. 'You're such a tease, Troy, I don't believe a word you say. My daughter is a child of today, I'm sure, far too sensible in her outlook to pander to the Victorian myth that all husbands are brutes and all wives submissive slaves. These days, girls go into marriage knowing their partners are human, beset by the same uncertainties as they are themselves. Modern man has no time for the passive, dependent, sexually repressed females of yesteryear. He expects his partner to be a buddy, a true equal who is prepared to share all responsibilities, including taking the initiative whenever she should feel like making love.'

This novel and rather daring aspect of marriage occupied Morva's thoughts during the hour she spent acceding to her mother's coaxing to dress for dinner in one of the many new gowns that had been carefully chosen to suit the stature and colouring of a girl whose childish build and features had indicated a definite tendency to develop along the same lines as her slim, attractive mother. Troy had been busy having a wash and tidy up in the bathrom that had been put at his disposal when she had chased her mother from the room, insisting she would manage without her assistance so that she, too, might enjoy an element of surprise when she judged the final results.

But when the time came to choose, Morva stood in front of the bulging wardrobe feeling bewildered as an urchin who had suddenly been called upon to step into the shoes of a spoiled princess. Hesitantly, she reached towards an off-the-shoulder ballgown in sequins and silk chiffon then drew back, deciding that it was much too elegant for such an informal occasion. She turned her attention to a slinky white sheaf of sequinned jersey but was frightened off by a plunging neckline that looked as if it might expose her navel, then dithered between a bright red, full-skirted dress with a romantic heart-shaped bodice and the blue printed silk which she eventually pounced upon when a glance at the clock told her that dinner was almost due to be served and any further delay might cause the impact of her transformation to be marred by Troy's hungry impatience.

It did not occur to her to wonder why she should be

thinking only of his reaction to her changed
appearance when she trembled into a dress that
seemed to heave a sensuous sigh as it slithered over
her head to writhe and cling around every curve until
it reached the arched insteps of slender feet strapped
into pearlised leather sandals with spiky heels that
held her teetering at least three inches above the floor.
The cut-away bodice swept over one shoulder, leaving
the other completely bare. A broad, frivolous ruffle, so
light it rose at the slightest movement, was positioned
like a sash across one shoulder while the rest of the
dress was left plain to display a design of clear bubbles
printed on a background of celestial blue that seemed
to become activated as she walked, creating the
illusion of an enticing, glossy-haired sprite raising a
naked arm and shoulder from a froth of sea foam.

Holding her candle to light her way she drifted
downstairs to the sitting room where the others were
waiting and hesitated on the threshold, fighting a shy
impulse to turn tail and run back the way she had
come. But the impulse was stifled by Troy's startled
exclamation.

'Good Lord, is it really Morva . . .!'

He put down his glass and paced slowly through the
gloom until his startled eyes leapt with the flame of
candlelight then darkened to a dangerous smoulder.
'Whatever happened to the cloistered virgin?' he
murmured so low that only she could hear. 'Such an
insinuating appearance could never be associated with
modesty. Dare I hope that at last you are feeling an
urge to try your wings, to escape from your cage of
Edwardian prudery?'

Then her mother's and Alan's praises intruded into
the magic moment, giving her no time to sift what she

felt could have been a very important message from his oblique remarks. All through dinner served in a candlelit dining room she pondered over words that appeared to indicate his complete agreement with her mother's earlier and very confident assertion that bridegrooms were as much in need of encouragement, as much a prey to doubt and uncertainties, as their young brides. She barely tasted what should have been a memorable meal of rich game soup and Scotch salmon soused in a creamy prawn sauce laced with brandy. Even the taste of plump, pink raspberries flambéd in Kirsch and served under a cloud of clotted cream failed to register on her tongue as she ate mechanically, wrestling with problems that increased the shadows cast by candlelight across the hollows and planes of her pale features.

It was a relief to agree when, shortly after dinner, as they were sitting around the fire listening to the sound of hail battering behind closed curtains and watching the spluttering of logs splashed by occasional drops of rain finding a route down ancient chimneypots, her mother broke the spell of contented silence by confessing with a barely concealed yawn.

'The excitement of today has left me feeling quite exhausted, does anyone else feel like an early night? How about you, Morva, dear . . .?'

'Yes, please.' She rose to her feet, conscious of Troy's eyes—smoky and potent as the peaty malt whisky gleaming in the glass that had been absorbing his thoughtful attention—following her movements.

She tried not to tremble as she accompanied her mother towards the door, but stumbled in her haste to cross the threshold when she heard her teasing reminder, 'Please, Alan, dear, don't keep Troy talking for hours, these two young lovers are still on honeymoon, remember!'

Her hands were still shaking when she slid the saucer-shaped holder containing the candle that had lighted her way upstairs on to a bedside table. A thrill of terrified anticipation lanced through her body as she stared down at the nest of peach-coloured sheets and lace-frilled pillows basking in the seductive glow of a flame flickering as frantically as the pulse in her throat, a signal of panic that had erupted the moment she began contemplating being drawn into shadowy, unknown depths of seduction, captivated by a desire—a hunger, almost—to satisfy the strange cravings and impulses that had been stirred into aggravated life by kisses dropped like crumbs to entice her step by cautious step in search of more.

Am I in love? she wondered, then realised in the second it took for her unzipped dress to fall to the floor that her entire existence had become dependent upon a body as tall and straight as fir trees that maintained a sturdy foothold on Canadian rocky mountains; upon a black fleece of hair shorn short to discourage a riot of ram-tight curls, and eyes so blue they astounded the senses, altering in shade according to moods ranging in temperament from the ice-cool glimmer of mountain glaciers to the brilliant warmth of cloudless, azure skies.

She sank slowly on to the bed, aghast by the discovery of a clause that had not been included in their contract, wondering whether a man who regarded his wife from a purely commercial point of view might accept love as an added bonus, or would decline what could quite fairly be judged emotional cheating. From a teeming confusion of thoughts one certainty emerged—she had arrived at a very important crossroads in her life, was being forced *now* to decide whether to remain on the straight, narrow route defined by her grandmother as female decorum, or to give in to a temptation to stray into unfamiliar territory, along a path strewn with pitfalls of doubt and fear yet one which her brave, unhappy mother had not hesitated to tread in her search for marital bliss.

The image that flashed into her mind of her mother's serenely happy features seemed to supply the answer she was seeking. She jumped to her feet and ran across the room to search the floor for the nightdress that had earlier been discarded, and found it shimmering in the shadows, a pool of satin and gossamer lace that caused her to gasp when she tipped it over her head to experience the shocking sensation of a fevered young body suddenly plunged into a depth of cool, clinging cream.

She was lying awake, her flame-flecked hair spread sultry as a web across a candlelit pillow when Troy walked into the bedroom. She saw the jerk of surprise that jolted him to a standstill and wriggled upright against her pillows, experiencing for the very first time the heady feminine satisfaction of seeing a self-assured male completely disconcerted.

'I lingered downstairs for as long as I could without arousing Alan's suspicions. Why aren't you asleep?' he accused, sounding acutely aggravated.

'I forced myself to stay awake because I wanted to speak to you in private,' she soothed, hoping to erase the scowl that seemed fair indication that he was in no mood to be reasonable. 'I see Alan has lent you a dressing gown,' she nodded towards the dark silk robe being mangled in a tightly bunched fist. 'I'll wait until you've changed, then we can talk in comfort.'

She slid down between the sheets to hide a smile of satisfaction when he stalked towards the bathroom, then flinched from the ferocity of his muttered curse when his head collided with a dangling lampshade fashioned from peach-coloured chintz into the likeness of an old lady's frilly mobcap.

The sound of a running shower seemed to go on and on for hours, giving her ample time to doubt the wisdom of her planned course of action, to regain lost confidence, then to doubt once again her ability to flirt with her husband, to convey without actually putting into words her readiness to enter into a much deeper relationship.

A mixture of fear, excitement and wonder at her own daring had driven fire into her cheeks by the time her much cooler, much calmer and vastly more self-possessed husband sauntered out of the bathroom. This time it was she who looked away from a damp brown body confined, but only just, within a rakish robe which six inches less of heavy black silk would have rendered positively indecent. She cringed, regretting the advantage he had gained from time, very conscious of a revealing depth of cleavage, a lace-edged plunge of cool cream satin down which his blue eyes slid and remained riveted. . . .

'Well, Morva,' he increased her inner turmoil by easing his rugged frame on to the side of the bed and placing a large flat palm flat down either side of her pillow, 'what is the subject you consider too important for its discussion to be delayed until tomorrow?'

All details of her carefully planned strategy became sunk without trace, confined to the depths of a mind completely seduced by the fascinating appeal of black, damply curling hair, blazing blue eyes and a whimsical mouth inching gradually closer.

'I was wondering . . .'

'Not again!' he groaned with mock dismay, then shrugged. 'Ah, well, at least to wonder is to begin to understand.'

She swallowed hard, convinced that she would never understand his complex nature—or the influence he exerted over her bewitched senses.

'. . . why didn't you prepare me for the reunion with my mother?'

She conquered an almost irresistible urge to clutch detaining fingers into silk stretched taut as a pelt across a broad width of shoulder when with a sudden frown he straightened and turned aside.

'Because you would not have agreed to a proposed meeting,' he charged truthfully. 'You are a robot, Morva, programmed to obey, to react only in accordance with the information fed into you. Perhaps now that you've sampled the self-confidence that can be derived from knowing you are loved without reservations you will never again be made to feel lonely or unwanted. If things should go wrong, if ever you should need an escape route, you'll have the security of knowing that there is love and comfort waiting for you here in your mother's home.'

If things should go wrong! What things could he have in mind? Had he arranged the reunion with her mother simply because *he* felt in need of an escape route—was this his way of easing her out of his life?

Loneliness and a sense of rejection had been her lifelong companions, yet fear of losing him cast a terrifying shadow over a future looming bleak as a tomb, a long, narrow void of dank hopes and stagnant promises. Desperation engulfed her shy timidity, spurring her towards a second courageous effort to put into practice sketchy, self-taught knowledge of feminine guile. Keeping her mother's confident assertions about the behaviour expected of modern-day brides firmly in the forefront of her mind, she swayed towards him until her cheek brushed against one silk-clad shoulder. Then she lifted fractionally away, hovering, indecisive as the moth fluttering around the flame of the candle that was casting seductive shadows over curves gleaming pale and creamy as the froth of lace and slender satin shoulder straps of a nightdress designed to entice a man's interest, to encourage him to discover by touch the tantalising secret of where cool, gleaming satin gave way to warm silken skin.

She sensed his startled immobility, the tense reaction of a virile body sensitive to inflammatory pressure, and dared to raise her head, offering warm, inviting lips to be kissed.

An aeon of uncertainty seemed to pass before he moved. Hesitantly, as if impelled against his better judgment, he drew her trembling body into a leashed embrace and began lowering hungry lips to claim her sweet, generous offering. A sob of relief and happiness clogged her throat as she savoured the precious moment, confident that overwhelming love would supply all the guidance needed by a novice eager to be taught lessons of love by a husband whose concern could move her to tears, whose strength and virility had carved a niche in her heart and stamped upon her mind an image of a tough, assertive, yet gentle giant.

'I can't thank you enough for all you've done for

me, Troy,' she whispered when his purposeful lips were a mere breath away. 'I'm so very grateful . . .!'

Immediately, as if shocked by the cold clarity of wintry mountain air, his hands froze to her shoulders and brilliant eyes darkened to the leaden hue of skies overcast by clouds gathering to unleash a growling tempest. Abruptly he released her, then, as if feeling a need for violent muscular action, he strode to grab a couple of spare pillows which he flung down upon the floor with bewildering savagery.

'What . . . what are you doing,' she demanded faintly, 'you're surely not intending to sleep down there?'

'Why not, I've slept in rougher places,' he clamped, spreading a peach-coloured blanket over a stretch of carpeted floor, 'and without the close proximity of a *grateful* young wife to raise my temperature!'

The sight of a doll dressed in satin bows and innumerable flounces propped up against her pillow seemed to incense him further.

'Please don't think that your attempt to carry out your social duties has gone unappreciated, Morva. *A child should never tell lies, speak only when spoken to, behave mannerly at the table, bestow a suitable reward for all favours!*' he mimicked wrathfully, 'it's just that I've always held the belief that gratitude makes a cold bedfellow!'

Darkness hid her shame when, without any visible wince, he pinched the candle's flaming wick between angry fingers.

'Goodnight, Morva,' he spurned coldly. 'If you should feel in need of a comforter, I suggest you cuddle your doll. Personally, I prefer to wait for passion to curl my toes!'

CHAPTER NINE

MORVA listened with relief to the bubbling call of a curlew gliding over its territory that seemed to be welcoming her back to wild, uninhabited, but blessedly familiar countryside. She drank in the sight of rounded fells ribboned with narrow silver streams, moors carpeted with purple heather whose new succulent growth had been carefully encouraged by frequent burning of old growth to enable new shoots and blown seeds to create ideal conditions for the pampered red grouse. Sheep dotted the fellside and grazed around a tarn whipped into waves by a gusting wind, and lower down the slopes, nestling at the foot of the hill, she caught a fleeting glimpse of the grey slate roofs of a house and outhouses belonging to one of the many tenanted farms that formed part of the Ravenscrag Estate.

As if the absence of traffic on deserted moorland roads had encouraged his attention to wander, Troy confided moodily, 'According to gamekeepers' reports, grouse shooting is likely to be patchy when the season begins. Apparently, an exceptionally wet spring held up the heather burning which encourages the growth of young shoots upon which the birds depend.'

'Gamekeepers are a notoriously pessimistic breed,' she told him diffidently, depressed by a certainty that she was very much out of favour with her morose companion. 'Just a few weeks ago they were bemoaning the fact that cold weather was preventing insect eggs from hatching, yet when the sun eventually began to shine the moors quickly came alive with the sort of insects fed to newly born chicks—especially daddy-long-legs which are considered to be a baby grouse's favourite titbit.'

'So you don't consider it likely that the shooting season will have to be postponed for a month, as has been suggested?' he queried, looking a little more cheerful.

Unwilling to dampen his hopes, to see the furrows deepening across his brow, she encouraged cautiously, 'I would hesitate to dispute the opinions of experts, nevertheless, each year for as long as I can remember I've seen gamekeepers shaking their heads and muttering into their beards about the scarcity of birds due to inclement spring weather, yet with unfailing regularity guns have been out as usual on the Glorious Twelfth.'

He acknowledged her sound reasoning with a grunt of satisfaction.

'There'll always be game wherever there's some wilderness left to breed, I guess. There was a time when the West's most magnificent beasts were hunted almost to the edge of extinction. The grizzly, the mountain lion, the elk and the bighorn sheep are now protected by law, so can roam freely around the wildest regions of the Great Divide country.'

'Sheep are regarded as big game?' Her note of surprise and the look she swept around fells dotted with the placidly grazing animals caused his lips to curl upward with amusement.

'The bighorn sheep is known to Red Indian hunters as the Lord of High Places because his natural habitat is high above the timberlands where its ability to bound over rocks and jump from ledge to narrow ledge has earned him the right to be counted among the world's most challenging and nimble-footed quarry. The rams are born bachelors who wander in carefree freedom until the December rutting season when they compete for a female's favours by fighting thunderous horn-to-horn battles, the victor claiming his choice of mate. Lately,' Morva became tensely attentive to his deliberately provocative drawl, 'I've begun wondering whether man has become over-civilised, too restricted and bound by rules of polite behaviour towards the opposite sex to enjoy the excitement of the chase, the thrill of combat, then the pleasure of mating which must be infinitely increased by the wild, sweet thrill of conquest!

'What sort of men do women really prefer, Morva?' Though his voice remained casual, when she looked up her startled brown eyes collided with a gaze that appeared intently interested. 'What choice would *you* make between a man who prefers to conquer and rule, and one who errs towards caution, deciding it is wiser to serve, even though he might lose . . .?'

Fed up with being tormented by unpredictable moods ranging from assertive to an uncertainty that was completely alien to the nature of a born manipulator, she told him tartly, 'I doubt whether metal in the process of being forged makes any distinction between pressure exerted by the anvil and blows administered by the hammer!'

When he continued driving in grim silence, offering no further comment, she tried to relax. But the moment she spotted the turrets of Ravenscrag poking above the skyline she became restless, nervously pleating the skirt of her dress as she prepared to face her grandmother, wondering how to explain her absence, how to combat the scandalised reaction, the recriminations and appeals to family loyalty, that were bound to follow any admission that she had spent the previous night under her mother's roof.

She remained unaware of Troy's quizzical glances, but could not fail to recognise exasperation in his tone when once again he displayed an uncanny ability to read her thoughts.

'Haven't you yet realised that you no longer have any cause to fear your grandmother's domination? That marriage has freed you from the tyranny of having to explain your actions, of having to beg permission to follow your natural inclinations? However reluctant your grandmother may be to relinquish her crown, she must be forced to abdicate in order to make way for the reigning Countess of Howgill. Power of authority is a responsibility that cannot be ignored and must always be exercised!' he stressed with an irritated snap that caused her cheeks to burn with humiliated colour.

But the crisis she had been dreading was postponed when, as Troy braked the car to a standstill at the end of the castle drive, Lynda ran bright-eyed with excitement down the steps to greet them.

'Troy, darling, I'm so glad you're home!' She stood on tiptoe to deliver a kiss of welcome which, to Morva's jealous eyes, appeared passionate enough to curl up the toes of even a bad-tempered grizzly. 'I've had a marvellous time in London,' she enthused, her lovely face glowing beneath his keen scrutiny, 'I can't wait to tell you all about it.'

'Hell, little sister!' Looking less complacent than she had expected, Percy strolled into view. 'Where the devil have you been—a simple 'phone call would have saved us a lot of unnecessary worry.'

'I wasn't worried!' Cheerfully, Lynda linked an arm into the crook of Troy's elbow. 'I knew she would be perfectly safe, any girl would be in such capable hands. Let's sit on the garden terrace.' She urged Troy forward. 'Percy, would you be a dear and ask Cook to prepare us a pot of her excellent coffee?'

Wishing she had yielded to the temptation to wear one of the many fashionable outfits her mother had insisted upon packing into a spare suitcase, Morva trailed miserably in Lynda's shapely wake, resenting the ease with which she was monopolising the attention of the man who supposedly regarded her as a sister yet whose amused blue eyes looked far from fraternal.

Obviously bursting with excitement, Lynda barely allowed them time to settle into chairs drawn up around a wrought iron table before spilling out a breathless catalogue of new experiences.

'Troy, I've attended the *swellest* parties, mixed with all the Best People in all the Best Places! Percy took me to the Henley Royal Regatta where we had Pimms on the lawn in the Steward's Enclosure, ate strawberries and cream for tea, then enjoyed a wonderfully childish night at the fair! And do you know what?' she appealed, wide-eyed with wonder. 'I sat side-by-side on the roundabouts with a real, live princess!'

'I don't believe it!' Troy's tone was so heavily laced with mockery Morva cringed, but Lynda was too carried away to notice.

'I did!' she nodded triumphantly. 'Also, every night we danced at a different, very exclusive nightclub, places with fantastic names such as Regines, Casserole, Legends and Tokyo Joe's, packed with grand people and well-known stars of showbiz drinking 'twenties cocktails and pink champagne! One of the very best parties,' she sighed ecstatically, 'was held in a hotel ballroom that had been transformed into a fairyland with tons of tinsel and glittering decorations, and with fountains rising and falling in time to the beat of heavenly music.'

'But it wasn't all play, remember.' Percy sauntered back on to the terrace. 'Have you forgotten to inform top management about the business deal I negotiated that will stamp the top people's mark of approval on Howgill Holiday, Inc?'

He sat down hurriedly, as if disconcerted by Troy's narrow, gimlet stare.

'As you appear to have adopted the role of negotiator on behalf of the company, the communication of facts must be your responsibility,' Troy charged. 'So, what is the deal and who are the people concerned?'

Morva felt resentment rising inside her as she watched her brother writhe, reduced to the level of a schoolboy miscreant called into the presence of a censorious headmaster.

He cleared his throat and with a dismal attempt to appear nonchalant airily outlined, 'Due to rapidly rising costs, fellow members of my polo club are looking around for alternative winter quarters for their ponies. During the season when they are needed as often as seven days a week to play practice chukkas and weekend matches, ponies must remain stabled at the club, but after skilful persuasion most of my friends have been sold on the idea of using Ravenscrag as a winter home for their mounts. Consequently,' he concluded with a burst of bravado, 'I have agreed to arrange a polo weekend on a date before the official opening so that interested parties can judge for themselves the standard of pasture and stabling facilities that are available.'

Even before he spoke, Morva knew that Troy's reaction to Percy's show of initiative would be negative. Consequently, her resentment seethed to boiling point when he vetoed it curtly.

'It's a great pity that you should have made such an arrangement without prior consultation, for I have no intention of allowing a horde of Hooray Henrys to trample muddy chukka boots over newly cleaned carpets, or to churn up the paddocks playing hockey on horseback. From next weekend onwards every available room in the castle will be occupied by overseas guests being charged a great deal of money for the favour of spending their vacations in aristocratic surroundings. So we have no need to court the patronage of your titled friends who, if rumour does not lie, will expect free board and lodgings in exchange for penning their titled signatures in the visitors' book.'

'But Troy, darling,' Lynda protested, her bedazzled eyes clouding with disappointment, 'you may be able to afford to be ruthless back home, but here success is measured by acceptance into the exclusive circle of high fliers that counts Percy as a member. Despite the fact that you are now an Earl in your own right, you have yet to be initiated into the rarified upper class atmosphere!'

Anger forked blue as lightning from his eyes when he pushed back his chair to condemn with amazed vehemence.

'Heaven forbid that my worth as a human being should depend upon acceptance into the snobocracy! My decision is final. No way will I put myself in the position of having to admit to a proud father that lack of vigilance on my part could be responsible for turning his usually level-headed daughter into a pathetic social climber!'

When he strode from the terrace with Lynda hurrying in his wake, obviously anxious to placate him, Morva's leaden spirits were not lightened by Percy's explosive observation.

'Belvoir is being deliberately bloody minded, not so much angry as dog-in-the-mangerish, I'd say! Lynda's obvious enthusiasm for London society has aroused latent possessive instincts he probably didn't realise were present until he sensed she was slipping out of his reach.'

She flinched from the lash of words delivered without thought for the hurt that might be inflicted upon a sister whose matrimonial bonds he had helped to knot.

'And *is* she slipping out of his reach?' she managed to enquire calmly.

'Not as yet,' he admitted moodily. 'As you've probably discovered for yourself, Canadian hillbillies are not the easy pushovers one might expect. I did my best to get Lynda chateaued—sloshed on wine— expecting her to jump at my proposal, but her giggling response was an evasive soliloquy about needing more time; not being rushed; having to speak to Troy before she could give me a definite answer. If you take my advice, Morva, you'll keep a sharp eye on your husband, for I'm beginning to suspect that Lynda may be biding her time and could still be harbouring ambitions centred upon the man she fell in love with long before his status was heightened by a title.' He jumped to his feet, exploding wrathfully, 'Though what she can see in that cussed, overbearing swine I simply cannot imagine!'

The sympathy he always seemed capable of arousing swamped her tender heart when he slumped back into his seat with his blond head bowed.

'What the hell am I to do?' he appealed to Morva. 'Because I relied too much upon your ability to exert influence on my behalf, I've allowed my friends to think that I rather reluctantly allowed myself to be persuaded to accept the post of social director in a subsidiary of my brother-in-law's huge international company, to assist him in his plan to utilise his inheritance by making Ravenscrag the nucleus of his company's first venture into the hotel business! As you can appreciate, within my elitist circle of friends the approved job circuit is strictly confined. Anything to do with manufacturing or industry is deplored as "brass with muck", but working for a company, and specially for a family business, is considered perfectly acceptable. But after spinning them such a tale—with the very best of intentions, mind you—I can't face the thought of being forced to give the chaps the big elbow, knowing that the outcome is bound to be total SOHF!'

'I beg your pardon. . .?' Morva looked as bewildered as she felt.

'Sense of humour failure,' he interpreted desperately. 'Please, Morva, can't you think of some way of helping me out, you must have some influence over your husband, especially after you and he have spent a clandestine night together.'

At the jab of his cruel finger upon the sore, tender spot she was nursing her face whitened.

'There was nothing secret or underhand about our absence,' she jerked. Then spurred on by an impulse to shock him out of his self-absorption she defied. 'We were in Scotland visiting Mother. Because a terrific cloudburst had made the roads impassable we were forced to stay the night.'

'Oh, really? And what did you think of her?' he enquired without the slightest hint of rancour.

'I found her radiant, extremely kind, and very charming,' she gasped, feeling the wind had been taken out of her sails.

'Yes, Mater's not a bad old stick. At least she can always be relied upon for the odd cheque or two whenever funds are running low.'

She shot to her feet, angered beyond belief by his blatant hypocrisy.

'Do you mean to say that during all the years you've spent agreeing with Granny's condemnation of our mother's character, helping to turn me against her, you've been in close touch—even accepted her money! Are there no depths you are not prepared to plumb in order to continue living a life of sybaritic idleness?' she condemned bitterly.

Nonchalantly he stood up to face her, severing their last remaining bond of affection with the unrepentant sneer.

'I have to fight dirty, to sink to the depths, as you so contemptuously put it, if I am to continue living the only sort of lifestyle I've ever known, because I resent having to learn obedience when I have been taught only how to rule. Nevertheless, my insincerity is not as great as your own, for at least I don't make promises

I'm not prepared to keep.'

'Promises . . .? Which promise did I make and fail to honour?'

'Come now, Morva!' he pretended to mock. 'You readily agreed how the cake was to be divided until all of it became *yours*!'

She backed away, deeply disgusted yet conscious of having suddenly been cured of physical and spiritual blindness, marvelling at all the things about him that she had not seen, all the faults and weaknesses that had remained hidden. How shrewd of Troy to have rated her brother lowly—how angered he would be if ever he were to discover the extent of the deception Percy was planning to impose upon his protégé.

Suddenly she saw herself as Troy would be bound to see her, a mute uncaring bystander—an accomplice, almost—to her brother's trickery. The thought was unbearable. Whatever the price, whatever the outcome, she had to prevent Lynda from being exploited, as ruthlessly manipulated into a loveless marriage as she had been herself. 'I'm prepared to bargain with you, Percy,' she blurted recklessly. 'Promise me that you'll leave Lynda out of your matrimonial plans and in return I'll make every effort to persuade Troy to offer you a more favourable position, preferably in his London office. Also,' she ran her tongue around lips that felt suddenly parched, 'I'll allow you to carry out whatever arrangements you have made with your friends.'

'You will . . .!' He sounded hopefully incredulous. 'But what excuse am I to use as a buffer during the inevitable collision with your husband?'

'All you need do if he should question your actions,' she husked, 'is tell him that I have granted permission—acting upon the authority he bestowed upon me and which he insisted had to be exercised.'

CHAPTER TEN

A COMPROMISE had been reached. Because the expected invasion of business executives had been postponed, moved to a later date, the sort of pressure Troy appeared to thrive on had been removed, so that the week prior to the arrival of their first contingent of overseas guests had been one of hectic preparation rather than the state of demented chaos Morva had envisaged. But her greatest release from tension had followed Percy's arrogant tilt at authority. Making no attempt to disguise his satisfaction, he had confronted Troy halfway through dinner with the complacent statement.

'Oh, by the way, Belvoir, as Morva has given the go-ahead to the business proposition I put to my polo-playing friends, all arrangements for their weekend visit have been finalised—except for their actual date of arrival. I was wondering,' he had paused to allow a few sips of wine to add to his moment of triumph, 'whether this weekend would be convenient?'

Inwardly, Morva had felt her courage shrivel, killed by the laser bright glance Troy had aimed in her direction. She had braced to endure a scene of humiliation, to have her first attempt to exercise authority contemptuously overruled by the hard-headed tycoon whose iron fist controlled the reins, determining every slight alteration in the progress of his company. But the expert manipulator, the boss man who had integrated the power of a lumberjack, the wiliness of a hunter, the skill of an angler into the jousting arena of commerce had donned the impassive mask of an Indian brave copying the possum's habit of avoiding confrontation by lying dormant.

'I hope you don't mind having your decision overruled by your partner,' Percy had dared to prod further, as if determined to elicit sparks from a smouldering furnace.

'On the contrary,' Troy had responded on a calm note of quiescence that had not deceived Morva for the briefest moment, 'I'm delighted to learn that my wife has begun acting upon her own judgment. As you both seem convinced that the polo-playing weekend is a good idea, perhaps we should include the sport among the programme of activities that has been arranged for the entertainment of our guests. But bear in mind, Eden,' he had concluded with the mildest of stings, 'that I'll expect to be provided with proof that your abilities can keep pace with your sister's assurance.'

Whether his attitude had been genuine or a mere front erected to deprive Percy of satisfaction, Morva had had no way of knowing. But the coolness with which he had treated her since, together with the amount of attention he was paying to Lynda, had convinced her that the only part she was to be allowed to play in his life was that of a walk-on, walk-off understudy. A role he had seemed to sanction when, after making several attempts to speak to him in private, she had finally run him to earth in his study.

Immediately, she had launched into an apology.

'Troy, I had a very good reason for siding with Percy. I'm sorry if——'

'So am I,' he had interrupted curtly, 'sorry you

appear incapable of transferring your loyalty from your brother to your husband. Percy's ambitions must mean a lot to you, otherwise you wouldn't have *dared*——'

He had broken off abruptly. 'Let's forget about it shall we,' he had returned to his papers with a weary sigh, 'there's no profit to be gained from raking over cold ashes. And please don't worry about having overturned my decision. So far as I am concerned,' he had dismissed contemptuously, 'any spark of spirit in a marble madonna must be counted as progress.'

And so Percy's friends had been invited to participate—though not to stay—in providing entertainment for guests who had been ferried in coaches that had swished their cargoes through deserted moorland roads, passed glowering fells and endless stretches of purple heather—scenery that had elicited exclamations of delight from Transatlantic visitors conditioned, by the need to live within handy reach of the hubbub of trade and commerce, to driving through crowded streets, breathing in air polluted by traffic fumes, noise, and odours rising from fast-food emporiums spewing out fuel needed to stoke up the boilers of human money-making machines.

'Excuse me, Lady Morva!'

Morva wheeled away from the window where she had been watching Troy marshalling an army of beaters and a variety of yelping, panting dogs into Land Rovers that were to spearhead the first day's attack upon plump, unsuspecting grouse.

'Come in, Mackay,' she encouraged the anxious-looking cook who was hovering on the threshold of a breakfast room whose sideboards were still waiting to be cleared of heated dishes that had kept a continuous supply of kidneys and bacon, sausages, kedgeree, kippers and scrambled eggs warm and moist beneath high-domed lids. 'Has something gone wrong, and if so, what can I do to help?'

'Nothing has gone wrong, Your Ladyship.' The cook seemed almost to bristle at the notion of anything daring to interfere with the culinary campaign she had entered into with the enthusiasm of a general determined to win a prolonged and exhausting battle. 'It's just that I've not yet been informed how many guests will be present at the picnic lunch. I must have some estimate of the size of the party, otherwise some of our guests may go hungry.'

'That is highly unlikely.' Morva had to smile when she thought of the amount and variety of food which for days past Mrs Mackay and her helpers had been busy preparing, stocking larder shelves and filling refrigerators and cold store to their utmost capacity. 'I have the list here.' She handed over a clipboard with a written list of names attached. 'Every one of our male guests is taking part in the shoot and quite a number of the ladies. I ticked off their names as they came down to breakfast and enquired which absent partners would be joining the picnic luncheon party. As you can see, I've made out a separate list of the less energetic who prefer to sleep late and eat lunch indoors.'

'Very sensibly, I dare say!' Her Granny's cut-glass accent tinkled behind Mrs Mackay's shoulder. She waited until Cook had bustled out of the room before sniffing haughtily. 'I've been amazed by the discovery that our grouse moors are about to be visited by a crude rainbow of colours! Never in my life before have I seen men assembled for a grouse shoot wearing loud checks and uniform jackets known, I believe, as windcheaters, coloured lime green, citrus yellow, purple and even a ghastly shade of pink. One would imagine they had come prepared to hunt parakeets on a tropic island,' she shuddered. 'The grouse will be frightened out of their wits by the discordant clash of colours long before they fall to the guns!'

Morva actually felt her cheeks draining pale when she spotted Troy's bulk looming on the threshold. He looked comfortably prepared to spend a day out of doors in a checked shirt, baggy guernsey, and the inevitable ancient jeans with legs tucked into a pair of dull green wellingtons. But his features, tanned russet as autumn beeches, set rigid with displeasure when he stepped near enough to overhear her Granny's disparaging remarks.

'May I remind you, Lady Lucy, that our guests are here to enjoy themselves and that it is in your own best interests to ensure that they manage to do so! Though they may not conform to the rules of dress laid down by one of your Victorian novelists who stated: *"I hold that gentleman to be the best dressed whose dress no-one observes"*, when it comes to rules governing shooting they all know the form. Each one is an experienced marksman, handpicked from an avalanche of applications from would-be guests because of reputations they have gained of being real dead-eyes. So far as I am concerned, the most important badge of membership required of any man about to take part in an exercise involving guns is skill and knowledge of how to avoid turning an enjoyable sport into a very dangerous hazard!'

Swiftly, as if denuded of patience, he swivelled twin bore attention upon Morva.

'We're almost ready to leave. Are you coming . . .?'

'No, I don't shoot,' she declined hastily, 'and besides that, I'll be far too busy supervising the picnic arrangements.'

She almost bit her lip with vexation, conscious that yet another opportunity had been lost, when Lynda's voice trilled from a close distance, 'Do hurry up, Troy, you're keeping everyone waiting!'

He turned to leave, then hesitated as if something about her woebegone mouth and slightly dejected-looking figure had disturbed his conscience. He frowned, then in a few lengthy strides drew near enough to tilt her chin with one forceful finger and to gaze long and deeply into wondering brown eyes.

'You've done a great job of work during the past few weeks, honey. I've heard nothing but praise from guests who believe in registering complaints whenever they are justified and in being equally quick to praise when they receive first-class treatment. Without exception, they appear to be charmed, if a little in awe, of your regal grace and quiet dignity. Some have even begun referring to you as "The Princess", did you know that?'

The pleased smile curling his lips had the instant effect of turning her knees to jelly.

'I must remember,' he mused with a hint of promise that caused her hopes to soar, 'to find some way of rewarding your tireless efforts. At the moment, however, duty calls.' With what she dared to imagine was a regretful sigh, he removed his propping finger from beneath her chin and stepped away. 'See you at lunchtime partner?' he cocked an enquiring eyebrow. 'Promise me . . .!'

'Yes . . . yes, of course.' She forced out the tongue-tied stammer while hammering heartbeats were drumming out the message that nothing on earth would keep her away.

But when he strode out of the room she was shot down to earth by her grandmother's sniping ascerbity.

'I am gradually being led towards the conclusion that your marriage to that young man was a great mistake. As we have all discovered to our cost,' she admitted grimly, 'he is far less malleable than we had hoped, much shrewder than we had expected.'

Walking stiffly upright she crossed over to the window to watch the cavalcade of Land Rovers moving away. 'I think, Morva, my child, the time has come when we must begin planning how best to rectify what, to modern-minded members of society, at least, is no longer regarded as an irreparable error.'

Morva's fingers faltered over the task of clearing and re-setting the breakfast table, ready for the small number of late risers who had refused to take up the option of having breakfast served in their rooms. Her spirits were still high, her heart and mind still occupied with Troy's image, his words and their possible meanings, yet the hard tone of her grandmother's voice intruded like a discordant note into her harmonious musing.

'I'm sorry, Granny, I wasn't paying proper attention, would you mind repeating your last remark?'

'I said,' she swivelled round from the window to face her, 'that it is time we began examining the possibility of your sueing for divorce. But we mustn't act too hastily,' she strolled nearer looking, to Morva's horrified eyes, like a thoughtful expert deliberating upon the next fraught move across the chessboard of *her* life. 'If we bide our time, I'm certain that Belvoir and his besotted young friend will provide us with all the evidence of misconduct we need to ensure a swift, uncontested suit and to make certain of a financially sound future for the innocent party. Meanwhile, we must begin preparing a rich, comfortable lining for your solitary nest by investing in as many pieces of jewellery, paintings and valuable *objets d'art* as your bank balance will permit.' Sharply she demanded, 'I trust you have been sensible enough to follow my instructions by insisting that your husband should provide you with a generous allowance in addition to the customary privilege of having personal accounts opened at all the major London stores?'

Morva stared, speechless with disgust, yet struggling to find excuses for the young, idealistic girl her grandmother must once have been, before a dutiful marriage had condemned her to a proud, ancient, *loveless* role in history. Pausing also to pity and to ponder for the very first time upon the feelings of her late and unlamented grandfather whose accident of high birth had sentenced him to be joined in matrimony with an eminently suitable partner fashioned from flawless steel by zealots devoted to the cause of ancestor worship.

'I could never do that, Granny,' she reproved sadly. 'Though Troy was generous enough to imply that the contract we entered into would entitle each partner to an equal share of company assets, I respect him too much to even consider abusing his trust.'

'Trust!' Her grandmother snorted inelegantly. 'You may sometimes feel inclined to forgive an enemy, but never to trust him!'

She drew herself up to her full, diminutive, yet intimidating height and with a lack of heat that betrayed complete faith in her ability to dominate, ordered complacently.

'You must be guided by my wisdom in these matters, my dear, otherwise I'll be led to suspect that you have been foolish enough to fall in love with the man! And while we are dealing with the subject of foolishness,' her voice sharpened, 'would you kindly cease denigrating your position by carrrying out menial tasks that are best left to servants!'

Every physical instinct responded immediately to her grandmother's command, yet simultaneously both mind and spirit were stirred from apathy into stubborn rebellion. Encouraged by the certainty that she was following in the wake of her mother's flight from a lifetime of total domination, she squared her shoulders, drew in a steadying breath, and severed the cords of bondage with the simple admission.

'If every fool wore a crown, then I should be able to satisfy all your ambitions by being made Queen! I am, in fact, two fools—one for loving and one for saying so. But perhaps it is an inherited weakness for, according to a quote by my mother from a treasured book of poems:

> "*All love is sweet,*
> *Given or returned.*
> *Common as light is love,*
> *And its familiar voice wearies not ever.*"'

A few hectic hours later, as she was being driven in the direction of a once-derelict cottage that had been transformed on Troy's orders into an ideal base for the last-minute preparation and despatch of picnic lunches, Morva's heady sense of freedom, her feeling of having shed an intolerable load, was intensified by the sight of parent kestrels hovering over fields in which hay was being turned and baled, waiting to pounce upon any disturbed mice or insects to provide a tasty meal for ravenous young chicks. Then as the road climbed up the side of the cultivated valley and clambered over the rim into an unbroken sea of purple moorland, a glimpse of red sandstone tower that could be seen from the fells for miles around reminded her of the church she had visited often as a child and where she had experienced a curious empathy with a trussed and bound figure imprisoned in ancient stone by some long-dead sculptor.

Subsconsciously, she began rubbing her wrists as if expecting to feel the weals of recently removed manacles, then feeling slightly foolish she leant her head sideways against the window frame of the car to cool fevered cheeks in a draught of air scented with heather, cool and pure as water surging and sparkling through becks draped like silver ribbons from the crowns of green, gently moulded fells.

Once she would have been devastated, reduced to a cowering mass of nerves by the scene that had followed her disclosure to her grandmother that she had been in touch with, and had even spent the night beneath her mother's roof. Yet she had survived the barrage of jealous outrage, her accusations of treachery and even her final, superbly acted display of tearful reproaches without suffering one iota of guilt, her tender heart protected from barbs by an armour of newfound confidence that had rendered it immune to the digs of family members who had manipulated and exploited her for their own selfish gain.

She winced when the distant sound of gunfire revived a childhood abhorrence of the acrid waft of spent cartridges and the sight of helpless birds being blasted in graceful flight, then plunging down to earth to be plucked into the jaws of slobbering retrievers and raced to enlarge macabre stoles of lifeless companions slung around the necks of the battalion of pickers-up that followed in the wake of victorious guns.

'It all seems such a dreadful waste.' Mrs Mackay put Morva's thoughts into words. 'All the work that goes into the rearing of birds, the cost of arranging a shoot, the need for expensive guns and cartridges, hardly seems justified when one considers the pitifully small value of the end product.'

Morva nodded agreement. 'Up gets a tenner, bang goes ten pence, and down comes a couple of quid, as they say, Mrs Mackay. Basically, it is enthusiasm for the sport and the pleasure men gain from outdoor activity that makes them argue that the expense is worthwhile.'

As soon as the estate cars laden with food and carrying the wives of estate workers eager to lend a helping hand drew up outside the one-storey cottage, Mrs Mackay took command, supervising the unloading of food containers, ushering everyone inside the one main room that had lanterns hanging from old oak beams, and piles of logs stacked against one wall ready to fuel an ancient iron stove which earlier in the day had had a fire kindled inside its iron belly that had been banked high then left to achieve a steadily glowing heat.

In a matter of seconds the room was transformed into a hive of activity. While Cook's Hunter's Stew—a savoury brew made from her own secret recipe—was being poured from containers into a huge black cauldron set on top of the stove, many hands were put to work at an old refectory table ranged down the centre of the room, slicing and buttering crusty, freshly baked loaves; unwrapping huge wedges of moist pungent cheese from protective veils of muslin; setting out trays with capacious earthenware soup bowls, spoons, and sets of salt and pepper, and lining others with rows of glasses ready to be filled with champagne from dark green, gold-foiled bottles ranged, still uncorked, along the cold stone floor of a larder.

Standing in the doorway of the cottage situated well behind the firing line, Morva caught an occasional glimpse of beaters' waistcoats flickering flame-bright among the heather; heard the far-off crack of unseen guns, yapping dogs, excited male voices, and shuddered from a mental picture of feathers cascading high in the air from a cartwheeling, bright-plumaged target. Then the signal for which she had been waiting rent the air, two long shrill whistles ordering all guns to unload before gathering to enjoy a welcome break and a substantial picnic lunch. During the short furore that followed handlers shouted urgent instructions to dogs sniffing nose-down through the heather in search of the fallen. Then silence fell as gradually the guns began drifting towards the cottage, their faces registering various degrees of pleasure or disatisfaction according to the number of birds they had bagged, exchanging good-humoured chaffing as they sank weary limbs on to travelling rugs spread across blanket of heather and waited for healthy appetites to be appeased by stew sending a rich meaty aroma drifting from the simmering cauldron.

Dogs were splayed out on the heather, contentedly

gnawing bones that had been salvaged the night before from the stock pot, and most members of the party were washing down second helpings of stew with glasses of chilled champagne by the time Morva's anxious eyes were rewarded by the sight of Troy and Lynda striding into view. In spite of her inability to dislike Lynda, Morva was shamed by a small thrill of triumph when she noted the bedraggled appearance of the girl who had made a picture of sartorial elegance when she had set out for the shoot a few hours earlier. Once-immaculate slacks had been ruined by grass stains and by mud clinging in patches to finely woven, creamy beige wool. A rent that had been caused by too-close proximity to thorny branches or prickly gorse bushes was visible on the shoulder of a superbly cut tweed jacket, and a felt hat with a row of tiny feathers stuck into its band, that had looked so perfect on Lynda's blonde head, had been reduced to a soggy mis-shapen pulp pinched between the fingers of a hand extended disdainfully, as if its owner was anxious to put as much space as possible between herself and the well-trampled, muddy-pawed object.

Keeping her movements casual, her expression unreadable, Morva hurried to offer refreshments to the exhausted-looking girl and her black-browed companion who appeared ready to inflict upon some unfortunate person the same force of action he had used to break the gun he had hooked over one arm.

'I've saved each of you a bowl of stew!' Keeping her eyes averted from Troy's scowling face, she spread out a rug on a patch of sunwarmed heather and tried not to sound too much like a nagging wife when she enquired. 'What kept you, the others arrived back ages ago?'

Looking on the verge of collapse, Lynda sagged gratefully on to the rug and immediately began undoing laces so that she could kick off a pair of soggy leather brogues.

'Why did no one warn me about the excruciating physical exertion required of a person wishing to be a mere spectator at a grouse shoot!' she wailed painfully. 'I did not come prepared to spend a whole morning walking up what appeared at first sight to be just a short climb, for stumbling over uneven ground, sinking into quagmires, or for having to balance for hours on a couple of rocking stones in a boggy butt accompanied by a man in the grip of grouse fever!'

The look of resentment she speared towards Troy explained much of her ill humour and sent Morva's spirits soaring. So far, Percy had kept his side of their bargain but his apparent defection had caused Lynda to seek consolation from Troy, demanding comfort and companionship which, up until this morning, had seemed to have been bestowed in abundance.

Even the arrival of two steaming bowls of stew did little to ease an atmosphere fraught with temper.

'You've allowed yourself to grow soft, Lynda,' Troy countered in a grimly unpenitent drawl. 'Attending lots of late-night parties, indulging your taste for cocktails and guzzling strawberries and cream are pastimes that are unlikely to prepare muscles for the strain of tramping over miles of moorland. Before repeating this morning's marathon, I suggest you take a leaf from Morva's book. Hours spent exercising Clio, together with an inborn timidity that leads her to emulate the custom of birds whose plumage enables them to fade into their background of rich brown earth and hazy blue heather, has endowed her with the

stamina and grace of a thoroughbred filly and the sort
of patient, noiseless presence that allows vixens to
approach a covey of game birds close enough to lift
sitting hens from their nests!'

Morva would have welcomed the phenomenon of
ground beneath her feet developing into a bog so that
she could have slid out of sight of azure blue eyes
making the most of their low vantage point by
commencing just about knee level to glint an
approving look over slender limbs that seemed poured
into a skin of pale blue denim stretched over thighs
slender as a youth's, then continued to confound such
a theory by curving outwards over rounded buttocks
then inwards to clutch a belt around the incredibly
slender waist of a figure that was deliciously and
unmistakably feminine.

She blushed scarlet, wishing not for the first time
that her mother's taste in fashion did not incline so
much towards the daring, the flirtatiously revealing,
then felt rescued from prolonged embarrassment by
Lynda's petulant remonstrance.

'You've scolded me once already for allowing my
fluttering scarf to frighten a covey of grouse off its
course, so please stop *nagging* me, Troy!' She thumped
her soup bowl down upon the ground and glared,
looking highly aggravated. 'And what is more, you
needn't preach any more about ethics of behaviour
that have to be upheld during a shoot, because I have
no intention of repeating today's harrowing experience.'

Angrily she appealed to Morva. 'What is it, d'you
suppose, about an apparently harmless pastime that
can turn a normally charming man into a boorish,
thoroughly disagreeable companion?'

A concerted shout of laughter from everyone within earshot caused Lynda's colour to deepen and a sheepish grin to lighten Troy's scowling features.

Nearby, a man chuckled. 'Good humour is the first virtue to perish on a game shoot. But in all fairness, I must admit that some of the dangerous tactics I've witnessed this morning could not help but rile a man such as our host who has proved himself expert at shooting down anything that flies.'

The chorus of assent that followed his remark seemed to indicate some source of annoyance threatening far worse consequences than the dispersal of grouse by a fluttering scarf.

'You can say that again!' A second man confirmed Morva's suspicions even before Troy heaved to his feet to extend a tight-lipped apology.

'I can assure you, gentlemen, that the errors of judgment encountered by most of us this morning will not be allowed to occur again. We are all aware that in order to shoot well, complete confidence in one's guns, cartridges, and companions is imperative. One bad cartridge out of a thousand is an occupational hazard. Everyone, at least once in his lifetime, discovers some fault with the mechanism of his gun. But no one, myself included, would be willing, or foolish enough, to risk a second involvement in a shoot containing a gun who has either forgotten or has never been taught the most elementary rules governing the handling and firing of guns.'

As if to confirm that the knot of trepidation tightening in her stomach had some connection with her brother's notorious uninterest in any form of sport involving travelling great distances on foot, Percy chose that moment to make his appearance. He

sauntered out of the cottage looking every inch a
country gentleman in tailored plus-twos, a husky, and
hand-made leather boots, and bearing a chicken
drumstick in one hand and a glass of champagne in the
other. Either oblivious to, or unaware of black looks
being directed by guests who began dispersing,
making no secret of their eagerness to be spared his
company, he sauntered on, alternatively nibbling and
sipping until he was near enough to boast.

'Not a bad morning's sport, wouldn't you say? All
due, of course, to my expert administration!'

'It depends,' Troy sounded dangerously affable,
'whether your aim was to kill grouse or to terrify
guests. You have a total lack of gun sense, Eden,' he
fired a quick snap shot that caught Percy point
blank with his mouth wide open. 'People like you
are a menace to companions on shoots. You do
realise that most of our guests have spent the
morning cowering in butts ever since they became
aware of a high velocity swarm of ammunition
coming from your direction? In future, to protect
your neighbours from yourself and yourself from
angry neighbours, you will not be allowed within
range of a rabbit on my estate!'

Percy's complexion turned puce. 'Are *you*,' he
placed insulting emphasis, 'daring to accuse me of
incorrect behaviour?'

'Social etiquette may be the prerogative of the
British aristocracy, but sporting etiquette is universal.
Nowhere are good manners so essential as in the
shooting field. Consideration for others is the
underlying principle, but any man who swings a gun
about regardless of where the barrels are pointing,
who climbs fences, and jumps ditches, without

breaking and emptying his gun is a danger to human life—a potential killer.

'There are occasions when it is permissible, even necessary, to carry a loaded gun,' Percy patronised, goading Troy's temper with an unpleasant sneer.

'And there are also rules governing such occasions, Eden,' Troy dismissed with the air of a man disinclined to waste time or energy upon cracking a nut with no kernel, 'just as there are rules governing employment which state that a man can be dismissed if his work should be discovered unsatisfactory.'

Morva clenched her fists, digging sharp nails into her palms without noticing the pain, conscious only that Percy, when provoked, could be savagely unpredictable.

'You can't dismiss me, Belvoir,' he swaggered, realising her wildest fears, 'my sister won't allow it! But in case you should be tempted to try, I must warn you that plans for a divorce are already under discussion!'

CHAPTER ELEVEN

IT was wonderful seeing Ravenscrag restored to its former grandeur, seeing valuables that had been packed and stored in a strongroom unearthed and rearranged in their original positions. Merely to dust them sent a thrill of delight through Morva's frame. Listening to her grandmother indulging in her self-imposed duty of conducting the uninitiated on a tour of the picture gallery, helping them to distinguish between Renaissance, Baroque and the rather more severe Byzantine style helped her to gain a faint insight into the mind of a stern matriarch who considered the aristocratic tradition of retaining wealth and position of far more importance than the mere bruising of human emotions.

As she stroked a duster across the elaborate gilding of a collection of Sèvres vases she paused, straining her ears to catch the comments of a group of guests whose voices were drifting into the State Music Room from the direction of the Painted Hall.

'*Don't you just adore being wakened each morning by a maid serving early morning tea?*' The questioner's voice rang with a note of awe.

'*Not half so much as I enjoy returning to my room after breakfast to discover that the bed has been made, the furniture dusted, and all discarded lingerie removed for hand washing.*'

'*Ah, yes, but you mustn't overlook the bliss of finding half a bathful of hot water drawn each evening—just waiting for the cold to be added—with a maid on hand to press whichever dress one has decided to wear at dinner!'*

'That meal is the highlight of my day! Delicious food expertly cooked and beautifully presented, and eaten in the company of a charming earl and his lovely young countess.'

Morva started with surprise, barely able to equate her personal estimate of worth with such a flattering description.

'I believe some extra special entertainment is being arranged for this evening to sort of compensate for the sadness of having to begin our journey home tomorrow. I've already booked our rooms for next year's vacation,' the voice faded as the ladies began moving away, *'my husband insisted . . .'*

Next year! Suddenly the colourful porcelain figure of Harlequin, the mischievous fellow supposed to have been invisible to all eyes except those of his faithful partner, Columbine, began dancing before Morva's tear blurred eyes. Where might Troy be a year from now? she wondered miserably. Would a combination of deceit, lies, and misunderstandings have driven him back home to Canada, to territory that was the natural habitat of Lords of High Places, born bachelors who treasured their freedom and relished the wild, sweet thrill of capricious, uncommitted conquest?

She screwed her duster into a ball and walked across to the window, conscious of the danger of blurred vision and trembling fingers spelling disaster to the fragile figurines she had made her own particular responsibility, unwilling to add to the mounting pile of breakages—shattered trust, ragged nerves, and an irreparably broken heart.

'Morva, honey, you do have a genius for hiding yourself away!'

She swung away from the window, feeling a sensation akin to relief as she welcomed a spate of Aunt Cassie's inconsequential chatter.

'As you are aware, Morva, Mrs Mackay has enlisted my co-operation with preparations for tonight's surprise Wild West Party. We are in complete agreement that the buffet meal should represent a last frontier of food to be savoured as it was in the past, before processed and packaged meals made recipes introduced into the Yukon by varied ethnic settlers all but obsolete. Our problem arose when it came to deciding which drinks should be served with the food. I reckoned that the traditional tipple of three or four shots of hard liquor per person would be all that was needed in the way of alcohol—even for the ladies, most of whom will have been raised on tales that made heroines out of high-kicking, hard-drinking gals who provided all the entertainment available in Wild West Saloons. But Mrs Mackay seemed scandalised by the suggestion and insisted that wine must be made available. So I've come to find out whether there is any unfussy, clean-flavoured Californian wine in the cellars?'

'I'm afraid I've no idea, Aunt Cassie, but either Troy or Percy should be able to tell you. Unfortunately, I'm not certain where either of them can be found at the moment. You could try the paddock where Percy may be finalising arrangements for polo matches that are due to be played this afternoon.'

'And what about Troy,' the old lady's voice held a gentle inflection which Morva's sensitive soul immediately interpreted as pity, 'have you no notion of his whereabouts?'

Find Lynda and Troy's sure to be around! she was tempted to blurt, but instead bit her lip and turned aside, anxious to hide her expression from astute eyes probing every unhappy feature. She started towards the door feeling trapped, sensing too late that Aunt Cassie's reason for searching her out had been no more than a ploy to get her on her own.

'Wait one moment, if you please, Morva!' The command issued in a tone of authority that had often quelled a canteen full of rowdy cowboys stopped her in her tracks. Reluctantly she turned, resigned to being browbeaten into betraying the cause of Troy's lengthy absences, solitary moods, and moments of deep introspection that were bound to spell out trouble to anyone who loved him. 'Sit down honey,' his aunt instructed more gently, 'and tell me what has gone wrong between yourself and my nephew. Don't worry,' she hastened to appease Morva's shamed gasp, 'the rift isn't obvious to everyone. But I know Troy better than most, which is why I reckon I'm entitled to demand from you the explanation he refuses to give. I'm on your side,' she coaxed urgently. 'Troy can be cussed, overbearing, bad-tempered as a bear, yet I know you love him as much as I do.'

Seconds later, without actually knowing how she had managed to get there, Morva was kneeling on the carpet with her head cradled in Aunt Cassie's lap, spilling out all her family's scheming machinations and the misunderstanding that had finally destroyed her marriage. Aunt Cassie listened in silence until she had finished, smoothing a comforting hand over softly tumbled hair, murmuring words of encouragement whenever broken phrases faltered, choked into extinction by bitter tears. Then after a while when tears had dried up and she had nothing left to say, Morva slowly raised her head and lifted wet lashes wondering why the old lady was doubtfully shaking her head from side to side.

'I'm sorry, honey,' she finally surprised her, 'but some of the things you've told me just don't add up. For instance, the reason Troy gave for proposing marriage strikes me as ludicrous. Why, in heaven's name, should a young man in his position—wealthy, attractive and with a horde of prospective brides to choose from—pretend to be in desperate need of the sort of guidance to be gained from a downy chick who would be hard pushed to find her own way around a chicken run!'

'Aunt Cassie . . .!' she gasped a protest.

'Morva, I hope you won't feel offended if I speak bluntly, because it's the only way I know how.' Doggedly she pressed on. 'Had my ex-tree felling, deer-stalking, trout-tickling, business barracuda of a nephew been in need of any sort of guidance he would have followed his usual practice of engaging an expert to teach him the tricks of the trade. Troy has always placed enormous value upon his freedom, so how can you possibly regard yourself as a bargain bride,' she snorted, 'when marriage has cost him his most treasured possession! No, honey,' she rejected firmly, 'far from shopping in bargain basements, Troy is attracted only by objects of refinement tucked away out of reach on the highest shelves. I fear your arguments must have been felled by his power of persuasion, that you have been played like a fish, stalked and led straight into a matrimonial trap—but for what purpose I cannot guess. Why not give him the benefit of the doubt,' she insinuated softly, 'by beginning to study the not inconceivable notion that my nephew's low-key, very hasty proposal might have been the act of a coward in love. . . .'

For the first time in days Morva's wounded mouth turned upwards in a smile as she considered the outrageous suggestion that Troy might be anything other than a dedicated go-getter, an assured, self-confident king of commerce, born to rule, to command respect from his kingdom of less ruthless, less determined, less single-minded followers.

'You can't be serious, Aunt Cassie!' She trembled as she dared to imagine for one fleeting moment what it might be like to be loved by Troy, to be swept into arms strong enough to afford hard-muscled protection against the assaults of her scheming family, to experience his stormy kisses and the electrifying touch that could unleash a tempest of feeling that only a man of force and ferment could satisfy.

She sighed, and with bright stars of wonder slowly fading from her eyes whispered sadly.

'Don't you think, Aunt Cassie, that anyone fortunate enough to earn Troy's affection would be left in no doubt about his feelings?'

'Ordinarily, yes.' Gently she smoothed a silken wisp of hair from Morva's brow. 'But you are far from ordinary, child, and I suspect that he could be a little in awe of you.'

'In awe of *me*!'

Aunt Cassie smiled. 'Honey,' she chided, 'I don't think you realise the impact your quiet, dignified manner has upon most people. Even I,' she confessed dryly, 'have sometimes felt tempted to curtsey when

entering the presence of yourself or your grandmother. Fortunately, I've been around long enough
to have learned that those who appear most self-
confident are often the most insecure. How is any
man to know, without the benefit of encouragement,
that the fragile porcelain shepherdess placed in his
clumsy keeping might possess as much tough
resilience as the roughly whittled image of an Indian
squaw?'

Urgently she tipped up Morva's chin until wise old
eyes were directly in line with bewildered brown.

'The choice is yours, Morva! It is up to you to take
the initiative, to prove to Troy that you are not a
brittle *objet d'art* but a flesh and blood woman with
enough passion in her veins to turn water into steam!
What do you say, gal. Are you game . . .?'

Swept along on the surge of Aunt Cassie's
enthusiasm, Morva gasped, drew in a shaken breath,
then stammered.

'Yes . . . yes I am! But how . . .?'

'I'll tell you how,' she beamed, her eyes flickering
bright with spirit inherited from tough, pioneering
ancestors. 'Just listen carefully while I explain exactly
what I want you to do. . . .'

For the remainder of that day guests seeking
information or advice from their polite, helpful hostess
found her unusually distrait, possessed of a dream-like
quality that made her responses abstract, her pale
pixie features turned fey by wide eyes that looked
stunned, fixed upon some mental vision whose bizarre
theme was holding her in the grip of horrified
fascination.

Conscious of a need to keep her mind upon her
duties, she made her way through the grounds towards

the building that was to be the base of this evening's festivities, the grand farewell party for their first contingent of overseas guests. Anxious to ensure that no curious follower should deprive fellow guests of the element of surprise, she took care to keep well out of sight of spectators crowding around the edge of the paddock waiting for the first polo chukka to begin. Her objective was a sizeable building set apart from the castle, a small private theatre that had been built by a previous earl who had indulged his thespian leanings by starring in plays and musicals put on by a society of amateur performers made up of family, staff, and any talent that could be culled from surrounding villages. Far from disbanding after the earl's death, the society had striven over the years to reach a standard of perfection Troy and his aunt had found amazing when they had eavesdropped on one of their regular weekly rehearsals and heard vigorous male voices belting out a rousing chorus from the musical *Oklahoma*.

It had been the colourful checked shirts, the high-heeled boots and wide-brimmed stetsons worn during the dress rehearsal that had inspired Aunt Cassie's idea for a Wild West Party. Her suggestion had been met with shy agreement from the cast, but when Morva stepped inside the theatre she was astonished by the discovery that enthusiasm whipped up by Aunt Cassie had resulted in the transformation of a rather bare oblong room into a replica of a Wild West saloon, complete with a long wooden bar well stocked with bottles ranging the width of a stretch of tarnished, fly-blown mirror; makeshift spitoons scattered over a sawdust carpeted floor; plain wooden chairs set around bare circular tables, and a honky-tonk piano placed in a pit situated directly below a stage draped with red velvet curtains.

Her heart soared, then plummeted to earth with the speed of a stricken grouse when she saw Troy, looking completely at one with his surroundings, one elbow propped against the bar as he listened without interruption to his aunt's flow of rhetoric.

'Can't you just *feel* the mounting build-up of atmosphere relevant to the hard-cussing, hard-drinking, hard-working era when men loaded with gold nuggets were prepared to fight each other for the privilige of twanging a chorus girl's garter?' Morva heard her exclaim as she approached the husband who had made it his business to ensure that they had not spent one moment alone together since Percy's spiteful disclosure.

'My only regret,' Aunt Cassie ran on, seemingly oblivious to the fact that her listener's grave attention had suddenly been switched to Morva, 'is that in order to preserve the element of surprise we could not be more explicit about the type of dress to be worn for the party. But I did my best to stress that outfits should be informal and I think my message was received and understood. However, just in case any of the guests should still be in doubt,' her brow puckered anxiously, 'you will remember, Troy, that you promised to get ready earlier than usual and remain where you can be seen so that your casual garb can be used as an example by doubters!'

She turned to smile acknowledgment of Morva's presence. Then with an air of innocence that caused Morva to wonder whether she had imagined the ruthless tactics that had been used to overrule all objections to her wickedly daring scheme, she promised.

'Tonight, I aim to serve everyone with a slice of history from the Canadian side of the family cake by trying to recreate the exact atmosphere and ambience prevailing on the day Troy's great-grandfather struck gold twice in one day—once by discovering a seam of precious ore in the mountains, and secondly by snatching from the stage of a rowdy saloon the shy young girl making her terrified debut before a pack of howling miners who was given just a split second to decide whether to say yes or no to his proposal that she should become his bride.'

A blast of noise almost drowned her final words, a nearby baying of masculine voices interspersed with excited yells and the rapid pounding of hooves, that had the effect of darkening the frown that appeared to have become permanently etched upon Troy's features.

'Let's hope the cake of history you are cooking up does not turn out to be little too authentic,' he warned grimly, stretching upright as if preparing to make a soft-footed retreat from a presence whose bowed head and nervously twisting fingers he found a source of aggravation. 'From what little I've seen of Eden's polo-playing cronies, there is little to choose between them and the irresponsible young braves who rode for hours astride galloping ponies, yelling blood curdling war cries to get the adrenalin flowing before embarking upon a frenzied massacre!'

Morva watched his stiffly upright figure until he had marched out of sight, convinced by his curt dismissal, by the angry set of his shoulders, of the utter futility of the plan to which she had been committed.

Desperately she swung round to appeal. 'Aunt Cassie, I can't do it——'

'You can and you must,' the old mind reader snapped before Morva had time to conclude her sentence. 'Troy is angry and miserable and you are to blame! If you place any value at all upon your marriage you'll sink your pride and seize what is likely to be your last opportunity to make him see sense!'

Feeling bullied beyond endurance, she hurried out of the old lady's presence. Much against her inclination, she was drawn towards the paddock where the hoots and howls of both players and spectators were growing louder by the minute.

The scene was riveting. Brilliant white shirts outstanding against a smooth sward of grass; lean, fit, arrogantly assured young men on thoroughbred ponies engaged in furious activity, uttering wild cries as they charged like knights of old waving sticks that whistled past their mounts' ears as they swung from the hips and leant well out from the saddle, striving to thwack a white plastic ball through goal posts situated either end of a long wide pitch. The exhilaration in the air was infectious. Bedlam reigned as the ponies exercised the unlimited stamina, staunchness, speed and natural balance that were the hallmarks of thoroughbreds. Excitement rose almost to the height of hysteria as admiring spectators applauded the bold approach, cool courage and arrogant disregard of watching strangers that stamped the players scions of aristocratic families.

The white ball bounded up the field. Without a touch of rein or spur a pony raced after it, enabling its rider to dribble it the length of the field towards the goal at full gallop. A roar of appreciation from the crowd set the pony dancing from side to side, then he lowered his muzzle to the ground as if bowing like a star performer acknowledging the applause of an admiring audience.

'Morva, isn't this great fun!'

She started with surprise when Lynda appeared at her elbow. Instinctively her eyes flew past her in search of Troy, but Lynda was alone, her beautiful face animated with excitement.

'Watch! Just look at Percy!' She dug sharp fingernails into Morva's arm, urging her to follow the progress of her brother who had the ball and was dribbling it towards the opposing team's goal. 'Ride Percy, ride!' Lynda almost screamed when an opposing back gave chase until he and Percy were riding neck and neck. Percy remained on the line of the ball, refusing to be ridden off, then a few yards from goal he flicked his wrist, tapping the ball straight through the centre of the goalposts. The sound of a whistle blown for goal was almost drowned by the cheers of his team mates who were circling around waving their sticks in the air.

'Goal!' Lynda shouted, almost overcome with joy. 'Well done, Percy, darling, well done!'

Morva's senses reeled, shocked by the message Lynda's words had communicated. Patiently, hardly daring to dwell upon the consequences, she waited until a pause ensued before the start of another chukka before beginning a cautious probing.

'I understood that Troy had persuaded you against becoming too involved with my brother.'

Lynda's brilliant blue eyes widened with surprise. 'Troy never interferes in business that does not concern him, surely, you know that! In any case,' she shrugged, 'my father has moaned to him often enough about how impossible I am to budge once I've made up my mind.'

'And have you made up your mind to marry my brother?' Morva forced out the faint thread of sound.

'I have,' she grimaced, 'but unfortunately Percy appears to have changed his.' Her lovely face clouded. 'Have you any idea why your brother has suddenly cooled off, begun avoiding me as if I were some sort of leper?'

Reluctantly Morva shook her head, unable to bring herself to voice an outright lie.

'Perhaps,' she husked painfully, 'Percy has become aware of your deep attachment to Troy.'

Lynda's loud peal of laughter was to reverberate through Morva's mind for hours afterwards.

'I did have a schoolgirl crush on your bad-tempered husband,' she admitted with a wide, engaging grin, 'but even I am not stubborn enough to continue competing in a race I've no chance of winning. But I don't mind admitting to you, Morva, that I intend playing every trick in the game to become part of all this.' Her wave encompassed the group of athletic young men, their strings of ponies, and Ravenscrag towering majestically in the background. 'Percy has introduced me into a world I find fascinating. He holds a key that can open a padlock, gaining me entry into the exclusive circle of jetsetters whose movements are governed by the months of the years—Barbados in January; Monaco in April; Gstaad in December. But each of us lacks one essential commodity—Percy needs money and I need style,' she admitted with engaging honesty. 'Therefore, how can either of us lose by combining our assets? Through marriage, we can wring every last drop of enjoyment out of his impeccable connections and my *embarras de richesses*.'

'Is that all you ask of marriage,' Morva's soft brown eyes pitied her, 'mere enjoyment?'

'Doesn't everyone ...?' Lynda looked genuinely surprised.

Impulsively, Morva swung on her heel and began hurrying towards the castle, her steps made urgent by the sudden realisation that if Lynda were prepared to strive so hard for so little, she would be a fool to allow shyness to prevent her from engaging in a no-holds-barred battle offering a prize to the victor that was worth so much. . . .

CHAPTER TWELVE

'AUNT Cassie, I can't appear in public wearing this!' Morva's protest faded into an appalled hush as she stared at her almost unrecognisable reflection in the mirror, feeling her stomach turning somersaults as she wondered what Troy's reaction would be to the shocking transition made by a timid brown sparrow into a bold, garish parakeet.

'You can and you must!' Aunt Cassie stepped back to admire the plume of ostrich feathers she had just finished pinning into an upswept coiffure. 'An hour spent acting the part of a voluptuous, thrill-seeking saloon girl is a preferable alternative to being condemned to sleeping for the rest of your life with only a doll for company,' she reminded tartly, and with what Morva considered to be unnecessary cruelty. 'Our object is to startle every man present with a nostalgic reminder of the busty, luscious young girls who descended upon the Yukon during the days of the gold rush, female prospectors who used sex appeal to send naughty thoughts racing through the minds of the miners they aimed to separate from their nuggets!'

Nervously, Morva blinked through a web of spidery, false eyelashes at the bright vermilion, tightly laced bodice squeezing her waist to the width of a man's handspan. Faint excitement began stirring beneath her terrified stupor as slowly she followed the course of hips curving seductively beneath a slick satin skirt that clung around slender thighs then flared towards a hem edged with black satin ruffles that rustled behind her knees when she walked then divided dramatically at the front to form a vee-shaped split deep enough to expose fishnet stockings topped with fancy garters and an enticing flash of bare thigh.

But would men's eyes remain lowered, she fretted painfully, or would they lift to linger upon a daring expanse of naked shoulders and curving breasts threatening to spill pale as cream from overfilled cups?

'Here, put this on!' As if Aunt Cassie had also begun doubting the wisdom of too much exposure, she hastened to fasten a diamanté collar around Morva's vulnerable young neck then stepped back, her gaze drawn as if magnetised towards a pointed pendant hanging like a warning to wandering eyes to avoid the hazard of venturing too far over snow white slopes, of risking a slide down a deep, mysterious plunge.

'Ah, well,' she shrugged, sounding suspiciously eager to appease an uneasy conscience, 'having gone this far, we might as well conclude the experiment. Just try to remember, Morva, honey,' she bolstered briskly, 'that the stage is set, the cast assembled, the audience primed to react with enthusiasm to the appearance of Klondike Kate. The success of the performance is entirely up to you!'

The escalating sound of raised voices, laughter, and enthusiastic applause which for the past hour had been encroaching upon the quiet, tense atmosphere inside the small dressing room seemed to bear out the truth of Aunt Cassie's words. Percy's friends, especially, sounded in high spirits, their unmistakably upper-class accents piercing the hubbub of excited Transatlantic voices.

'Good luck, gal!' Aunt Cassie stood on tip-toe to press an encouraging peck upon Morva's brightly rouged cheek. 'Try to forget for an hour that you are the Countess of Howgill. Go in there with both guns blazing—a Diana of the mountains determined to get her man!'

She urged Morva along a deserted passageway then with a last quick wink of encouragement opened the door, stepped inside the makeshift saloon, and left her standing alone, reeling from a blast of noisy merriment—high-pitched female laughter; snatches of song; the thumping beat of a honky-tonk piano; the tinkling of bottles and glasses, and a fug of tobacco and alcohol fumes that caught in her throat and set her senses reeling.

She drew in a steadying breath, trying to pluck up sufficient courage to embark upon the act that was to be the culmination of Aunt Cassie's endless rehearsals, then stretched out a hand and with the fluttering apprehension of a nervous patient about to enter a dentist's surgery, flung open the door and stepped over the threshold into the din and furore, the rowdy, exciting, flirtatious cut and thrust of the Naughty Nineties.

Everyone present appeared wildly determined to enter into the spirit of the recaptured era. Guests who had copied Troy's casual attire of checked shirt and denims were seated around tables with prettily flushed wives perched upon their knees. Flamboyantly dressed members of the Dramatic Society were encircling the piano, belting out a lively, slightly ribald chorus. Percy's friends had obviously taken full advantage of the free drink made available all evening and looking decidedly tipsy, swaying shoulder to shoulder around a table laden with tots of hard liquor and singing at the tops of their voices. Even Troy, standing alone at one end of the bar frowning moodily into an untouched drink, seemed to epitomise the dejection of a miner with nothing to celebrate, one whose pick had bitten into a seam of fool's gold.

Suddenly she found it surprisingly easy to follow Aunt Cassie's hammered-home instructions to adopt the stance of a flirtatious coquette. She draped her surprisingly relaxed body sideways against the door jamb so that her shapely silhouette was boldly outlined, bending one knee until it was thrusting provocatively through the slit in her skirt to provide an eye-popping display of black stocking top, pale thigh, and garish garter. Immediately, she was spotted by one of Percy's friends whose loud, appreciative whistle drew all eyes towards her.

'I say,' she heard him yell, 'who's the libidinous lady in the doorway? Excuse me, plebs, while I go and share her space!'

Morva's brightly painted smile slipped a little when he rose to his feet and began lurching towards her. Then the air became rent with the whoops and yells of followers surging in pursuit, copying the foot-tripping, elbow-digging, shirt-grabbing stampede of miners determined to stake first claim to a gold mine. In seconds she was cornered, fighting off ardent hands, nauseated by a whisky-fumed breath that murmured, 'Come and have a clutch, my saucy beauty!'

'Stop it! Leave me alone,' she cried out in fear of being crushed by a tightening circle of jostling young sportsmen with senses inflamed by a surfeit of alcohol.

'My God, *Morva* . . .! No, it can't be!' Percy's

shocked cry of recognition penetrated the din. She saw his pale face wavering as he tried to fight his way towards her before it disappeared completely behind a barricade of muscular shoulders.

'Gerroff, I saw her first!' When more hands reached out to grab her she began fighting like a hellcat, kicking, slapping, gouging the ring of leering faces.

'My Gawd, she's got spirit!' Someone yelled on a note of exultant laughter. 'Let's toss her aloft, men, until she's willing to concede a garter as a prize to the lucky winner!'

She screamed, feeling clutched by an octopus when hands snapped around her waist, her arms and even behind her knees. All hell seemed to break loose as she fought off her good-humoured attackers. She heard the crack of splintering wood above the sound of their laughter; women's screams, and the shattering of glass as if someone had been pushed into violent collision with a drink-laden table. Then miraculously pressure began easing as faces were plucked rapidly one by one from out of her line of vision. Gripping fingers relaxed until only one pair of hands remained to swing her vigorously off her feet upwards until she felt pinned against a heaving, muscular chest, stabbed to the heart by a glare of azure blue anger.

She slumped in his arms, too terrified to speak to her rock-jawed husband as he strode out of the chaos-filled saloon and carried her with less concern than he would have shown to a disjointed doll across the moonlit gardens, into the castle, then up the staircase leading to their suite of rooms. Once inside, he dropped her on to the canopied bed then stood towering, his features at one with the slit-mouthed, snarling-toothed images of dragons peering down with contempt upon the most flushed, dishevelled creature ever to have disgraced the stately marital bed.

'I suppose,' Troy accused in the manner of a man determined to keep tight control of seething emotions, 'there must be some explanation for your shocking behaviour, but for the life of me I can't even begin to imagine what impulse could have driven you to appear before guests dressed like a caricature of some brazen Yukon hussy, to incite drunken horseplay, and to encourage—no, *invite*—the attentions of a crowd of unruly, witless youths! Are you so resentful of having been forced into marriage,' he scathed, 'that you are willing to go to any extreme that might shame me into agreeing to a divorce?'

She shrank small when his towering frame lowered towards her, afraid of the terrible anger she sensed was boiling beneath a clamped-down lid of control. She parted parched lips to deny the accusation but found that words would not be forced through her tight throat. Then to her horror she felt tears pricking behind her eyelids. His angry image wavered as tears welled then balanced for a second on mascara-spiked lashes before falling with a plop on to rouged cheeks. Momentarily her vision cleared, then quickly she lowered heavily shadowed lids to shut out the sight of eyes of flashing dangerous ice-blue sparks.

His grip upon her shoulders caught her completely unawares. She was jerked from the bed, planted on her feet, then force-marched towards the bathroom.

'I refuse to watch you weeping with all that muck on your face!' he gritted, opening the door to shove her in the direction of the shower cubicle. 'You can undress in there,' he nodded towards opaque glass screens, then stood implacable as a rock with arms folded across his chest directing a look that seemed designed to shrivel the despised outfit from her shivering limbs. 'Toss that odious costume over the screen, I'll be waiting here to dispose of it!'

Afterwards, she was never able to decide how she managed unaided, with shaking fingers and in such a confined space, to unfasten hooks and unbraid laces until the outfit he found so offensive slithered from her limbs to gather in a limp, gaudy heap around her ankles. Yet she could never forget the relief she found in tears that washed her empty of grief while needles of warm water rinsed soapsuds from her face, clearing her skin of every last vestige of make-up, her hair of every last trace of lacquer.

But her worst moment arrived when she turned off the shower, then stood pink and glowing with embarrassment wondering if he had carried out his threat to remain.

'I've finished . . .' she finally quavered, then felt her heart respond with a bump to his curt reply.

'Good, then I suggest you come out and get dried.'

The thought of stepping completely nude into his line of vision suffused her body with a blush of humiliation, but he had left her with no alternative. Tentatively, she eased an inch-wide gap between sliding glass doors, then swallowed back a sob of relief when she saw him standing facing in the opposite direction with one arm extended backwards, dangling his towelled dressing gown within her reach.

Thankfully, she made a grab and shivered inside its immense folds, then felt immediately soothed, comforted as a child cradled within familiar arms.

'Thank you, Troy.'

Interpreting her words as permission he turned

round to stare silently, motionlessly, and with a deep intensity that jolted her sensitive nerves and raced scorching colour to her still-damp cheeks. Then casually, as if his volcanic emotions had been doused to the point of extinction, he reached for a towel and began calmly drying her hair.

'Troy,' she pleaded, completely fooled by his air of mild uninterest, 'I have never plotted behind your back. Divorce was entirely Granny's idea, and though you must have thought me disloyal when I granted Percy permission to carry out the arrangements he had made with his friends, I did so with the best of intentions. He had made up his mind to marry Lynda,' she gulped, 'so I attempted to spare you unhappiness by making a deal—permission to carry out his plans in exchange for his promise not to try to manoeuvre Lynda into a marriage of convenience.'

'As you have been manoeuvred.' His response sounded grim, but the steady stroking motion of the towel did not waver. 'Lynda is no fool, she's too much her father's daughter ever to enter into a contract containing detrimental clauses. And as for your brother . . .' Though the towel was obscuring her vision, she sensed that his lips had thinned. '. . . I can think of nothing I would enjoy more than seeing him installed in the executive suite of his father-in-law's company where he'd be worked harder than any packhorse and, at best, be allowed two or three days off in a year. So you see, Lynda's circumstances are in no way parallel with your own. She is no little lost cub, totally unprepared to face the world—and especially not the world of men—being callously used as bait to attract any prowler likely to fill her family's empty larder!'

His wrist snapped the towel away from her face to allow him to study her flushed, tousled bewilderment.

'You were handed to me on a plate, Morva, and much as I despised your family's greed my will was too weak to fight the urge I felt to offer you protection, to restore your surroundings to the standard of perfection necessary to display to advantage the highly polished facets of a flawless gem.'

She stared transfixed, wondering which was the more preferable—being recruited as a partner in a business deal, or being acquired in the manner of one of the status symbols all business tycoons seemed to find essential and which they were apt to list under the heading of legitimate expenses. Something seemed to snap inside her head. Flinging caution to the winds, ignoring every lesson she had ever been taught about decorum, dignity, and the need to preserve a ladylike composure, she stamped an enraged foot and flared.

'I don't *want* to be treated like a priceless heirloom stuck way out of reach, protected from rough handling by a glass case, you ... you ... *great blind bear*!' Too furious to care about the voluminous robe sliding fast as melting snow from her heated body, she charged forward to pummel his chest with angrily bunched fists. 'I'm a flesh and blood woman,' she stormed, 'just aching to become a wife!'

His reflexes reacted with the pouncing leap of a virile mountain ram responding to the call of his mate. She suffered just one second of stunned immobility before his arms snapped around her naked body to draw her willingly into a baptism of fire and flame.

Hard, hungry lips stamped her mouth with his fiery brand of possession as she thrilled to the urgent yet restrained grip of hands tempted to crush, but mindful of the fragility of their precious burden. Desire rippled through his powerful frame as he swept her off her feet to carry her out of the hot, steamy bathroom towards the cool silken sheets of a bed that enclosed them like a lair.

'I love you so much . . . I've waited so long . . .' he groaned, brushing aside a scented mane of hair that was preventing his lips from nuzzling the tender creamy slope of her shoulder.

She turned in his arms and on a soft breath of wonder severed his last remaining strand of restraint.

'Dearest Troy my own Lord of High Places, I thought I'd never hear you say those forbidden words . . .!'

Pale fingertips of dawn had begun poking their way between a gap in dark red curtains when langourously she stirred.

'Troy,' she dared to tease with the confidence of one certain of the sort of answer she would receive from a husband who was lazily anticipating a revival of spent passion by kissing and stroking his way up her captive body, 'you must feel as cheated of profit as grouse shooters who spend a fortune in the pursuit of small, useless creatures?'

His black head jerked up to direct an azure blue shaft of indignation. Then swiftly he retaliated against the mischief in her smile by gathering her softly quivering body into tender, wonderfully protective arms.

'The world of commerce revolves around the

premise that there is nothing on earth that cannot be bought—at a price,' he husked through a throat tight with emotion, 'but you may rest assured, my darling, that I would not accept a gold mine in exchange for my adorable bargain bride!'

ROMANCE

Variety is the spice of romance

Each month, Mills & Boon publish new romances. New stories about people falling in love. A world of variety in romance – from the best writers in the romantic world. Choose from these titles in December.

FOR ADULTS ONLY Charlotte Lamb
FLIGHT TO PASSION Flora Kidd
DOLPHINS FOR LUCK Peggy Nicholson
NO HOLDS BARRED Jessica Steele
A CHANGE OF HEART Sandra Field
THE DEVIL'S PAWN Yvonne Whittal
ONE LAST DANCE Claire Harrison
TROPICAL EDEN Kerry Allyne
HEIDELBERG WEDDING Betty Neels
LOVERS' KNOT Marjorie Lewty
RAGE Amanda Carpenter
BRIDE BY CONTRACT Margaret Rome

On sale where you buy paperbacks. If you require further information or have any difficulty obtaining them, write to: Mills & Boon Reader Service, PO Box 236, Thornton Road, Croydon, Surrey CR9 3RU, England.

Mills & Boon
the rose of romance

ROMANCE

Next month's romances from Mills & Boon

Each month, you can choose from a world of variety in romance with Mills & Boon. These are the new titles to look out for next month.

LOVE GAMES Charlotte Lamb
WHAT YOU MADE ME Penny Jordan
NO HONOURABLE COMPROMISE Jessica Steele
NO GENTLE PERSUASION Kay Thorpe
TOTAL SURRENDER Margaret Pargeter
DARK NIGHT DAWNING Stacy Absalom
SECRET FIRE Violet Winspear
RAGE TO POSSESS Jayne Bauling
HUNT THE SUN Margaret Way
DRAGON'S POINT Claire Harrison
MAN AND WIFE Valerie Parv
NO MAN'S POSSESSION Sophie Weston

Buy them from your usual paperback stockist, or write to: Mills & Boon Reader Service, P.O. Box 236, Thornton Rd, Croydon, Surrey CR9 3RU, England. Readers in South Africa-write to: Mills & Boon Reader Service of Southern Africa, Private Bag X3010, Randburg, 2125.

Mills & Boon
the rose of romance

Best Seller Romances

These best loved romances are back

Mills & Boon Best Seller Romances are the love stories that have proved particularly popular with our readers. These are the titles to look out for this month.

THE BRIDE OF THE DELTA QUEEN
by Janet Dailey

SONG OF THE WAVES
by Anne Hampson

FORBIDDEN FIRE
by Charlotte Lamb

NIGHT OF LOVE
by Roberta Leigh

Buy them from your usual paperback stockist, or write to: Mills & Boon Reader Service, P O. Box 236, Thornton Rd, Croydon, Surrey CR9 3RU, England. Readers in South Africa write to: Mills & Boon Reader Service of Southern Africa, Private Bag X3010, Randburg, 2125

Mills & Boon
the rose of romance

Mills & Boon

Take 4
Exciting Books
Absolutely
FREE

Love, romance, intrigue... all are captured for you by Mills & Boon's top-selling authors. By becoming a regular reader of Mills & Boon's Romances you can enjoy 6 superb new titles every month plus a whole range of special benefits: your very own personal membership card, a free monthly newsletter packed with recipes, competitions, exclusive book offers and a monthly guide to the stars, plus extra bargain offers and big cash savings.

**AND an Introductory FREE GIFT for YOU.
Turn over the page for details.**

As a special introduction we will send you four
exciting Mills & Boon Romances Free and
without obligation when you complete
and return this coupon.

At the same time we will reserve a subscription to
Mills & Boon Reader Service for you. Every month
you will receive 6 of the very latest novels by leading
Romantic Fiction authors, delivered direct to your
door. You don't pay extra for delivery — postage and
packing is always completely Free. There is no
obligation or commitment — you can cancel your
subscription at any time.

You have nothing to lose and a whole world of
romance to gain.

Just fill in and post the coupon today to MILLS & BOON
READER SERVICE, FREEPOST, P.O. BOX 236, CROYDON
SURREY CR9 9EL.

Please Note:- READERS IN SOUTH AFRICA write to
Mills & Boon, Postbag X3010,
Randburg 2125, S. Africa.

FREE BOOKS CERTIFICATE

To: Mills & Boon Reader Service, FREEPOST, P.O. Box 236,
Croydon, Surrey CR9 9EL.

Please send me, free and without obligation, four Mills & Boon Romances, and reserve a
Reader Service Subscription for me. If I decide to subscribe I shall, from the beginning of the
month following my free parcel of books, receive six new books each month for £6.60, post
and packing free. If I decide not to subscribe, I shall write to you within 10 days. The free
books are mine to keep in any case. I understand that I may cancel my subscription at any
time simply by writing to you. I am over 18 years of age.

Please write in BLOCK CAPITALS.

Signature _____

Name _____

Address _____

_____ Post code _____

SEND NO MONEY — TAKE NO RISKS.

Please don't forget to include your Postcode.

Remember, postcodes speed delivery. Offer applies in UK only and is not valid
to present subscribers. Mills & Boon reserve the right to exercise discretion in
granting membership. If price changes are necessary you will be notified.

6R   *Offer expires December 31st 1984*